CLAIMING HIS NINE-MONTH CONSEQUENCE

CLAIMING HIS NINE-MONTH CONSEQUENCE

JENNIE LUCAS

MILLS & BOON

First published in Great Britain 2018
by Mills & Boon, an imprint of HarperCollins*Publishers*
1 London Bridge Street, London, SE1 9GF

Large Print edition 2018

© 2018 Jennie Lucas

ISBN: 978-0-263-07378-2

MIX
Paper from
responsible sources
FSC® C007454

This book is produced from independently certified FSC™ paper to ensure responsible forest management. For more information visit www.harpercollins.co.uk/green.

Printed and bound in Great Britain
by CPI Group (UK) Ltd, Croydon, CR0 4YY

To Pete: my hero today and every day.

CHAPTER ONE

ARES KOURAKIS!

As rhythmic music and lights pulsed across the dark, hot dance club, the whispers of his name grew louder, building to a roar. The famously handsome Greek billionaire had come to Star Valley at last.

Ruby Prescott rolled her eyes at all the excited chatter and awed stares being directed toward the shadowy VIP section. A handsome billionaire? Yeah, right. In her experience, billionaires were always ugly—if not on the outside, then definitely on the inside. No man became that rich without seriously warping his soul.

But she had more important things to worry about. Bartending was Ruby's third job today, after a morning teaching skiing to four-year-olds and an afternoon working at a clothing boutique. She couldn't stop yawning, and she still had a whole night of work ahead. Stretching to wake herself up, she moved across the bar, pouring drinks as quickly and carefully as she could.

"Ares Kourakis," one of the waitresses, Lexie, breathed across the bar. "Can you believe he finally came?"

"It would be stupid if he didn't, after buying a house here." Ruby had been on that house's cleaning crew, too, six months earlier, right before the man had bought it for the reported sum of thirty million dollars. Nice place, if you liked your ski lodges fancy and as big as a football stadium. Pouring another beer and setting it on the bar, Ruby said sourly, "And what kind of name is Ares, anyway?"

"He's so handsome and rich, he can have any name he wants. I'd be Mrs. Ares Kourakis in a second!" Staring toward the dark corner of the bar, Lexie fluffed up her hair. "I'm so lucky he's sitting in my section!"

"Very lucky," Ruby replied sardonically, "since I heard he just broke up with his girlfriend."

"Really?" Lexie's face was ecstatic. Unbuttoning another button on her white shirt, she picked up her tray and hurried toward the VIP corner.

Ruby continued to pour drinks behind the bar. The Atlas Club was busy tonight, the last night of the March film festival that made the town even more crowded than usual.

Billionaires weren't unusual in Star Valley, a ski-resort paradise in the Idaho mountains and a playground for the rich and famous. The busiest time was Christmas, when wealthy people brought their families to ski, and July, when the famous McFallon and Company CEO conference caused a fleet of private jets to descend on the valley like bloated metal vultures blocking out the sun.

But Ruby knew, just as there was no such thing as free drinks, there was no such thing as Prince Charming. The richer and more ambitious a man, the darker his soul.

Another waitress hurried up breathlessly to the bar. "I need three mojitos, one no sugar, one pomegranate, one extra lime and she said if the mint isn't muddled right, she's sending it back."

Ruby sighed. At least wealthy men, unlike their girlfriends and wives, generally stuck to ordering uncomplicated drinks, like scotch on the rocks. Turning away, she swiftly made the cocktails. As she placed them on the tray, Ruby saw a young blonde in a tiny red dress trying to inconspicuously scoot past the bar.

"Ivy?" Ruby said incredulously.

Her nineteen-year-old sister flinched, then turned. "Um. Hi, Ruby."

"You can't be in here! You're underage! How did you get past the door?"

Her cheeks flushed red. "I, um, told Alonzo that there was an emergency with Mom, and I had to talk to you."

Panic went through Ruby. "Is Mom—"

"She's fine, I swear. She was sleeping when I left." Ivy squared her shoulders. "But I heard Ares Kourakis is here."

Oh, no. Not her little sister, too. "You can't be serious!"

"I know you think I'm just a kid. But I have a plan." Ivy lifted her chin. "I'm going to seduce him. All I have to do is poke a few holes in the condom, get pregnant and he'll marry me. Then our troubles will be over."

Ruby stared at her sister in shock. She couldn't believe what she was hearing. "No."

"It will work."

"You'd risk getting pregnant by a man you don't even know?" she gasped.

Ivy narrowed her eyes. "I have a chance for everything I ever wanted, and I'm going to take it. Unlike you. You keep talking about your big dreams, but you don't *do* anything! You're just a coward!"

Staring at her little sister, Ruby caught her breath, feeling like she'd just been punched. *You're just a coward...*

"I'm going to live the life of my dreams," Ivy continued. "No more worries about bills. I'll have jewels and live in a castle." She looked at her elder sister contemptuously. "Maybe you've given up on your dreams, Ruby. I haven't."

Five years younger than Ruby, Ivy had always been the spoiled baby of the family. But looking at her now, in a tight red dress and stiletto heels, Ruby realized with a chill that her sister had grown up to be freakishly beautiful. She might actually have a chance to succeed at her awful plan.

"Don't do this," she breathed. "I can't let you do this."

"Try to stop me." And Ivy disappeared into the crowd.

For a moment, Ruby couldn't move. Exhaustion, shock and fear, never far away since their mother's diagnosis, clouded her vision like too many punches to the head.

Ivy's plan to trick Ares Kourakis into marriage was just a joke, surely. Her little sister had always been allergic to hard work, but even Ivy wouldn't sell her body—her *soul*—to a man she didn't love just because he was rich!

Would she?

"Wait," Ruby cried, and started to follow her, only to crash into the other bartender, causing an empty bottle of vodka to fly off the shelf and smash to the floor behind the bar. As the other bartender cursed loudly, she heard laughter and mocking applause from patrons at the bar.

"What's wrong with you?" Monty, the other bartender, hissed.

Heart pounding, Ruby wordlessly grabbed a broom and quickly cleaned up the glass. She turned to Monty. "Cover me."

"What? Girl, are you crazy? I can't take over all the—"

"Thanks." With an intake of breath, she headed for the darkest corner of the bar. A chill went down Ruby's spine at the memory of her baby sister's voice.

All I have to do it poke a few holes in the condom, get pregnant and he'll marry me.

Squaring her shoulders, Ruby strode toward the VIP section. Up on the platform a few feet above the rest of the club, past the man's glowering bodyguard, she saw her sister in the bright red dress, already ensconced cozily at a table with a brutally handsome dark-haired man. Ares Kourakis.

As if the Greek billionaire felt Ruby's gaze, he turned.

Dark sardonic eyes glittered in the darkness, cutting through her. She felt a flash of heat. Catching her breath, she shivered with a strange fear. Even the man's name was dangerously sexy, starting with the Greek god of war and ending with a kiss.

She shook herself. What was wrong with her? She mocked her body's reaction. The rumors about him were true. The man was handsome. So what? It just meant he'd be even more selfish. Even more heartless.

She wasn't going to let him ruin Ivy's life, and possibly a baby's.

Tightening her jaw, Ruby went grimly forward.

Ares Kourakis, thirty-six-year-old billionaire, sole heir of the Kourakis shipping fortune and the most famous playboy on six continents, was *bored*.

He surveyed the dance club. Even here, in the remote mountains of the American West, he was bored by the same old expensive scotch, the same old pounding electronic music, all boringly unvaried from Stockholm to Singapore.

All the women in dance clubs were exactly the same, too. Oh, their looks varied, of course, as he traveled around the world. But the *type* of girls in clubs was always the same: model thin, model beautiful, perfectly made up with long hair, short skirts and high heels.

And whether their eyes were brown or blue or black or green, they always glittered with the same hunger: willing to do anything—be anyone—to possess him.

His money. His status. His body.

That last one, Ares usually hadn't minded so much. He generally took advantage of whatever was offered as casually as another man might enjoy dessert after dinner. He didn't feel guilty, either. Gold diggers knew what they were doing. They hoped to lure him through sex into the permanent misery of marriage. But he knew how to play the game. He lazily enjoyed the sensual delights when they were offered and just as quickly forgot them when they were not.

Ares was good at the game. For many years, he'd enjoyed it. Until recently.

He'd been so busy over the winter, traveling constantly to get a new business acquisition under control, that he'd been unable to even visit the luxurious ski lodge he'd purchased in Star Valley months before. He'd thought he might enjoy having a place to relax, far from the demands of New York. But as was typical, after buying it he'd been too busy to use it. Then his mistress, Poppy Spencer, had begged him to accompany her to the Star Valley Film Festival, where she'd secured a viewing of her first film.

Poppy was beautiful and tiny, blond and glamorous, in her midthirties. A trust-fund baby, she'd never had to work and floated through potential careers, quitting whenever they got boring or difficult. Last year, in the middle of all the awards-season parties in Hollywood, she'd decided she should be a movie star. Declaring auditioning as "tedious and embarrassing," she'd financed a movie herself, as the writer, producer, director and sole actor. Three hours long, filmed as a monologue in black-and-white, it was a hugely important film—Poppy had told Ares so repeatedly. In fact, as they'd flown to Star Valley on his private jet a few days before, she'd groused that this tiny film festival wasn't big enough for her groundbreaking artistic achievement.

Poppy had been mortified last night when her film had been roundly panned—even booed—by the audience. Weeping profusely at his ski lodge afterward, she'd demanded that he fly her immediately to Nepal, so she could "disappear forever." She'd paused midsob, brightening as she mused the possibility of hiking to the top of Mt. Everest alone, thereby becoming a famous mountaineer.

When Ares had declined to drop everything and fly her to Nepal, she'd accused him of being unsupportive of her dreams and broken up with him. She'd left Star Valley in such a huff, she'd even been willing to fly economy class.

But Ares had stayed. He'd just gotten to Star Valley. He liked the little town, and he'd barely spent any time at his brand-new house. He hadn't even had a chance to snowboard, and though the late-March sun was swiftly melting the snow, he wanted at least a few hours on the mountain, damn it, before he headed for Sydney tomorrow on business. Why on earth would he go to Nepal? Especially since he knew within months Poppy would announce she hated mountaineering and instead wanted to be a forensic anthropologist like some character on a TV show?

Poppy could be occasionally amusing, and was

good in bed. More important, she'd never made emotional demands, never asked him about his childhood or appeared interested in his thoughts or feelings unless they related to her. She was strictly surface level, which suited him perfectly. With his busy schedule, they'd often gone weeks without speaking to each other between social events.

Ares suddenly realized he was glad she'd left last night. He'd been bored a long time. Not just with Poppy, but with everything. Everyone. He'd spent the last fourteen years turning the shipping empire he'd inherited at twenty-two into a vertically integrated worldwide conglomerate that sold and shipped everything from minerals to motor oil. Kourakis Enterprises was the love of his life. But even his company had somehow lately become… uninteresting.

Grimly, Ares tried to push away the feeling. He'd spent today on the mountain as he'd wanted, with the bright sun, melting snow and icy wind. But even that hadn't been as enjoyable as he thought it would be. He'd heard his name whispered wherever he went. Women skied into his line of vision, giggling and tossing back seductive glances, cutting him off and forcing him to change his path so he didn't crash into them or veer off into a tree. He'd ended the day more irritated than he'd begun.

So tonight, his last night in Star Valley, he'd decided he needed to go out. Perhaps his mood would improve after a passionate encounter with some attractive woman he'd never have to see again.

But now, as Ares looked blankly across the VIP table at a young blonde telling some long, boring story, he knew he'd been wrong.

This had been a mistake. All of it. He should just go. Leave for Sydney tonight. Tomorrow, he'd tell Dorothy to put the ski lodge back on the market.

"Excuse me," he said curtly, startling the blonde in the middle of a sentence. He tossed money on the table to pay for the single glass of scotch, barely tasted, left here a few minutes ago by the vapidly smiling waitress. Looking away, he started to rise.

Then he froze.

Across the club, he saw her.

Time seemed to slow around him as a jolt of electricity went through his body. The flashing lights, thumping music, frantic dancers all became just noise, mere smudges of color. Only she was in focus. *This woman.*

Not a woman. *A goddess.*

Glossy dark hair tumbled over her shoulders. Her

eyes were dark and huge, fringed by thick black lashes. Her full, heart-shaped lips were deep red.

She was dressed differently from the other women. Instead of tight, short, low-cut clubwear, she was innocently sexy in a simple cotton gingham top, sleeveless and secured with a casual tie at the waist. It caressed the hourglass curves of her body, from her full breasts to her tiny waist, expanding to full hips sheathed in feathery-soft jeans.

And the goddess was coming straight for his table.

Ares's throat went dry.

Straight for him.

His bodyguard stopped her at the bottom of the stairs. It was only when she turned to speak to Georgios that Ares felt able to breathe again.

The young blonde at his table had continued chattering nervously about something or other. He'd forgotten she was there. Sinking back into his chair, he said abruptly, "You should go."

"Go?" The blonde gave a foolish grin. "You mean to your place?"

Not listening, he made a rough gesture to his bodyguard, who let the gorgeous brunette pass.

Dark-haired and sloe-eyed, the goddess climbed the few steps toward him. He stared at the sway of her hips. What was it that drew him? Her earthy sex appeal in those seemingly modest clothes, like a 1940s pinup? Her incredible body, her soulful eyes?

Whatever it was, she drew him like a flame. Boredom was suddenly the last thing on his mind. His breathing was hard as she came forward. And not only his breathing.

But the brunette barely looked at him. Instead, she turned accusingly to the blonde girl at the table.

"All right. Let's go."

The girl, who suddenly looked defiant as a teenager, snapped, "You're not the boss of me, Ruby!"

Ruby. A beautiful fairy-tale name for a woman who looked like a brazen princess who could tempt any man into eating a poison apple. Ares didn't mind her possessiveness, not in this case. It was all he could do not to push the other girl out of the chair himself. But he forced himself to say courteously to the blonde, "Yes, you need to go. I'll be glad to buy your drinks for the night, but—"

"Drinks?" Ruby turned her angry glare on him. Ares felt the same jolt, the one that left him electrified and breathless. "My little sister is underage, Mr. Kourakis. How dare you offer her alcohol?"

"Your sister? Underage?" Frowning, Ares looked at the blonde girl, then back at the goddess. She stood over the table in a fury, taking quick breaths. Understanding dawned. "Is that why you came up here?"

Ruby scowled. "Believe me, I'm doing you a favor, Mr. Kourakis. Ivy had this *fantastic* idea of seducing you and getting knocked up so you'd marry her."

Ares's jaw dropped; not at the plan, but at the honesty.

"Shut up!" the girl yelled. "You're ruining everything!"

"She wanted to marry a billionaire. Any billionaire would do." Looking at him, Ruby tilted her head, her expression almost contemptuous. "Please excuse her for being stupid. She's only nineteen."

The look she gave him spoke louder than words: *What kind of man your age would date a teenager?*

She made him feel ancient, at the age of thirty-six.

"I hate you!" the blonde cried.

She turned sharply to her sister. "Ivy, go home.

Before I have Alonzo toss you out so hard, you bounce on the sidewalk."

"You wouldn't dare!" But looking at her, Ivy's defiance fled. "Fine!" Rising to her feet, she stomped away.

"And don't even think about telling Mom what you tried to do!" Ruby yelled after her. She glanced back at Ares, humor curving her deliciously full lips. "Sorry for the interruption, Mr. Kourakis. Have a good night."

As she turned to leave, he grabbed her wrist.

Her skin was soft and caused heat to flood through his body. He heard her intake of breath when he touched her.

Ares looked up at her. "Wait."

"What do you want?"

"Have a drink with me."

"I don't drink."

"Then what are you doing at a bar?"

"Working. I'm a bartender."

She worked for a living? He looked at her capable hands. "Take a few minutes. Your boss will understand."

Her frank dark gaze locked with his. "No."

Ares frowned. "Are you upset because I was talking to your sister? I was never interested in her."

"Good." She pulled her wrist from his grasp. "Please excuse me."

"Wait. Your name is Ruby? Ruby what?"

Glancing back, she gave a low laugh that he felt all the way to his toes. "There's no point in telling you."

"But you know my last name."

"Against my will. Everyone is talking about you. Apparently you're quite a catch." Her voice was sardonic.

Ares had never been brushed off so thoroughly by any woman. He tried to understand. "You are married?"

"No."

"Engaged?"

"I'm *working*." She enunciated the word as if she thought maybe he'd never heard it before. "And the waitstaff will be needing their drink orders."

Ares stared at her. "You would truly rather work than have a drink with me?"

"If I'm not pouring drinks, it hurts everyone's tips. Which hurts everyone's ability to pay rent. Not everyone," she added sweetly, "owns a thirty-million-dollar house bought with cash."

So she'd noticed his house. Even the price. Encouraged, he stretched out his arm suggestively along the top of the seat next to his. "Most other women would quit their jobs on the spot to spend an evening with me—"

"So have a drink with one of them," she said, and walked down the steps without looking back.

Ares sat for several moments in stunned silence, alone at the VIP table. He dimly heard the thumping music. He barely noticed as women in tight dresses and stilettos continued to parade below the platform, dancing provocatively for his benefit. He glanced over at Georgios. His bodyguard rolled his eyes. Exactly what Ares was thinking, too. Same music. Same club. Same people.

With one exception.

Who was this Ruby, and why could he suddenly not imagine any outcome tonight that didn't end with her in his bed?

Rising to his feet, Ares told Georgios, "You can go."

His bodyguard brightened. He was probably thinking of calling his wife back in New York, who was no doubt up late with their new baby. "Should I leave the car?"

"I'll find a ride home. But tell the pilot I want to leave first thing in the morning."

"Of course. Good night, Mr. Kourakis."

Turning, Ares stalked through the nightclub. Dance music pounded in waves, colored lights blurring in the dark, sultry heat as crowds of people parted for him like magic. Men looked at him with envy, women with desire. But he had only one object. One goal.

When he reached the bar, a free chair immediately appeared for him, as such things always did. He slid into it as his due.

Ruby looked up from where she was pouring drinks behind the bar. Her lips parted in surprise, then annoyance. "What are you—"

"Tell me your last name."

"It's Prescott," a waitress said nearby. At her glare, the girl continued in a squeak, "Ruby Prescott."

At last they were getting somewhere. Tilting his head, Ares said, "Nice name."

"I don't think you can criticize," she snapped. "What kind of parents would name their child after the Greek god of war?"

"*My* parents," he said flatly. He changed the subject. "I'm bored with scotch. I'll have a beer."

She blinked in surprise. "A beer?"

"Whatever you have on tap."

"Not some expensive forty-year-old scotch? Just regular old beer?"

He shrugged. "I don't care what it is. As long as I'm having that drink with you."

Ruby scowled, and quickly poured him the cheapest beer, making sure to leave lots of foam. Taking the glass, he slugged back a long gulp, then wiped the foam from his mouth. "Delicious."

Her scowl deepened as she turned away, moving around the bar, fixing drinks with impressive speed. He could see why she dressed in a sleeveless cotton shirt. The club was warm, and she moved so swiftly from the bottles to the well drinks, grabbing glasses and ice, it was almost athletic.

Ares nursed his beer, watching her work. Her full breasts were spectacular, yes, but every last bit of her was amazing. His gaze traced appreciatively over her softly curved arms. Her backside was nicely curved, too. He'd never seen any woman with such an hourglass shape, and her bottom was something a man could really hold on to. He nearly groaned at the erotic images that suddenly filled his mind.

But it wasn't just her curves. Ruby Prescott had other, more subtle charms. Her thick black lashes, now fluttering with irritation against her pale skin. The tremble of her lips, ruby red like her name. She frequently bit them in concentration as she worked.

His eyes traveled over the sweep of her long hair, dark as a raven's wing, tumbling down her back. The curve of her bare shoulder. The angry gleam of her dark eyes, which suddenly met his accusingly.

"Why are you doing this? Is it some kind of game to you?"

"Why?" he asked, sipping his cheap beer. "Is it one to you?"

"If you think I'm playing hard to get, you're wrong." Standing directly in front of him on the other side of the bar, Ruby glared. "For you, I'm *impossible* to get."

Her expression was fierce, her dark eyes glinting like a lightning storm over a dark ocean. Her chest rose in quick, angry breaths. She didn't even realize her beauty, he thought. She had no idea. And unlike everyone else in the world, she wasn't at all impressed by him.

And in that moment, Ares knew he had to have her.

Tonight.

Whatever it took.

Whatever it cost.

He would have her.

CHAPTER TWO

WHAT WAS THIS stupid Greek billionaire trying to do?

Ruby's body felt strangely tight as she turned to pour a drink. She could feel his hot gaze trailing over her body.

She couldn't imagine why a man like Ares Kourakis would be paying attention to her. He could have any woman here—starlets attending the film festival, ski bunnies, rich debutantes just in from the French Alps. He couldn't possibly be interested in a regular girl like Ruby.

But why else would he be sitting at the bar, not looking at anyone but her and meekly drinking the worst-tasting beer in the world?

She couldn't think of any other reason.

People were starting to notice, too. Monty and the waitstaff were constantly sneaking glances while the female customers sitting at the bar looked as if they'd happily stab her with their olive picks.

Ruby served up two gin and tonics, a screwdriver

and a rum and Coke, then turned on him angrily. "Seriously," she hissed, bending closer over the bar. "What is your problem?"

Ares's gaze bored into her. "You."

"Me? What did I do?"

"You're the most desirable woman in the club. You fascinate me."

She saw the dark hunger in his eyes. A flash of heat traveled through her body. She had little experience with men, but she would've had to be blind not to see that he wanted her.

Her gaze traced over him. The hard edge of his jaw, rough with five-o'clock shadow. The rough curl of his short dark hair. The rhythmic thrumming of his powerful fingers against the wood bar. She was aware of him in a way she didn't want to be. Aware of everything, even the way her own knees felt suddenly weak beneath her.

He'd caused that just by looking at her. Just by telling her she was desirable. She'd thought she couldn't fall for any rich man's charm. That she was too smart to fall for it.

But was she? She felt strangely intoxicated, though she hadn't had anything to drink. She felt like she was in a dream, though she was awake. This man, so handsome, arrogant and wealthy—

so out of her league—had made just the barest effort and her whole body quivered, as if on his command.

What was wrong with her?

And, oh, sweet heaven, what would it do to her if he actually *touched* her?

What would it feel like if he lifted his hand from the bar and stroked her cheek? If his fingertips traced down her throat? If he cupped his hand gently around her breast?

Ruby's nerve endings zapped with shock, her nipples tightening beneath her cotton bra. A sweet low ache coiled low and deep inside her. She put her hands on the bar to steady herself.

"What…" The words caught in her throat, and she swallowed, her voice suddenly shaky. "What do you want?"

His dark gaze fell to her lips. He smiled.

"Dance with me."

Dance with him? This Greek god whom everyone else was losing their minds over? Ruby caught at the tendrils of her sanity. "No."

"Why not?"

Don't ever believe anything a rich man tells you. Her mother's sad voice came back to her. *They are liars, all of them. Liars and thieves.*

Taking a deep breath, Ruby squared her shoulders and managed to say in a calm, strong voice, "I don't dance."

"You don't dance? You don't drink? You *are* old-fashioned." His eyes slowly traced her body, making her cheeks hot in spite of herself. "I could teach you," he murmured. "When is your break?"

She gripped the edge of the bar. "No, thanks. I just work here. It's not what I do for fun."

Ares tilted his head thoughtfully, taking a sip of his beer. "What do you do for fun?"

"I…" Ruby tried to remember. It had been a long time since fun was on her agenda. Even before her mother got sick, before Ruby had taken three jobs to provide for their family, she'd been busy after school, taking care of Ivy and running the house, back when their mom was the one who'd worked three jobs. Ruby blinked. Fun?

Ares covered her hand with his own.

"Tell me what you'd do." His voice was low, persuasive. "If you could do anything in the world tonight."

At the touch of his powerful hand over hers, a tremble went through her, as violent as a hard flood of rain across hot, parched earth. A bead of sweat formed between her breasts.

How could he make her body react like this just by putting his hand on hers?

Pulling away, Ruby muttered unwillingly, "I'd be up on the mountain."

"The mountain?"

"Some of the other ski instructors are running Renegade Night."

"What's that?"

"There's no night skiing at the resort, so before the season ends, just when the snow's starting to melt, we run our own the old-fashioned way. To-night's the last full moon."

"Is the moon so bright?"

"We also use torches."

Ares's eyes sharpened with interest. "I've never heard of it."

"Of course you haven't. It's locals only."

"I see." Finishing the beer, he put the glass down on the bar. "Good to know. Thanks for the drink."

Tossing a twenty-dollar bill on the bar, Ares left without another word.

Ruby stared after him, her mouth round with surprise. All she'd wanted him to do was leave her—and Ivy—alone. But now he had gone so abruptly, she felt oddly deflated.

"Wow." Monty, the other bartender, snorted beside her. "That was cold. What did you say to make him practically turn and run?"

Ruby's cheeks went hot. She quickly turned to restock the clean glasses. "He just wanted a beer."

"Obviously."

A waitress hurried up with another drink order. Dazed, Ruby poured three shots of tequila, and had just put them on the tray when the lights of the club suddenly turned full-on. She blinked, blinded by the bright light. There were groans of shock across the crowd as the music, too, was turned off.

Paul Vence, the wizened former musician who owned the Atlas Club, appeared on the dance floor in all his purple-leather-wearing glory.

"We're closed for the night," his voice boomed, surprisingly loud for a man so short. "Everyone out!"

The customers and the staff looked at each other in bewilderment.

"Out! Now!" Mr. Vence looked at the bartenders and staff. "Don't worry. All of you will still get paid for the night. Tips included."

The staff brightened considerably. "Shall we start cleaning up?" Lexie asked.

"It's been handled. You can all just go." His beady gaze focused on Ruby. "Especially you."

And with an intake of breath, she knew.

Tell me what you'd do. If you could do anything in the world tonight.

Ruby felt a tingle at the back of her neck as customers slowly started to file out, muttering and moaning. With the lights on so brightly, the club looked plain, with bits of trash on the floor. The men suddenly appeared disheveled, their clothes wrinkled; the women had smudged mascara and tired eyes. The illusion was over. The magic of the nightclub—the music, the darkness, the flashing colors—was gone.

The waitstaff, on the other hand, were practically singing with joy in the changing room, chattering happily about how they'd spend their unexpected free night. As Ruby went back to retrieve her coat from her locker, she lingered, waiting until the others had left. She tried to tell herself she was crazy. Imagining things. There were plenty of other possible explanations.

But as she left the Atlas Club, he was waiting for her, as she knew he'd be.

The sidewalks had already grown quiet on the snowy street, as the last of the clubgoers and staff disappeared in the cold night to the nearby Settler, called the Sett for short, or other bars in the tiny mountain resort town.

Ares Kourakis was leaning against a streetlight, dressed in black, surrounded by snow. Butterflies filled her belly at seeing him.

"You did that, didn't you?" she said accusingly.

Ares gave her a careless smile. "What if I did?"

She shook her head. "The club would have made a fortune tonight. How much did you pay Mr. Vence to close?"

"It doesn't matter."

"And you made sure the staff had the night off. Paid. With tips and everything."

"I knew it would kill your pleasure if they didn't."

Ruby's voice croaked as she asked, "But why?"

"I told you." He came closer beneath the street lamp, until their bodies were only inches apart. With his greater height, he towered over her. She squared her shoulders desperately beneath her vintage jacket, refusing to back an inch, but she couldn't hide the rapid rise and fall of her breath. Reaching down, he tucked back a tendril of her long dark hair. "I want to be with you tonight."

Be with her. Be with her? Looking up, she tried to glare at him. "Do you always get what you want?"

His dark gaze poured through her soul. "Yes."

She swallowed. "But—but why?" she whispered. "Why me?"

"I told you. You're incredibly beautiful."

"Most of the girls in the club were way prettier than me."

His expression changed. "You're different."

Ruby shook her head helplessly. "Different how?"

"You weren't trying to get my attention."

Ah. Now she understood. She felt suddenly, incomprehensively disappointed. She wasn't special after all. Somehow he'd almost made her hope—

Cutting off the thought, she lifted her chin. "So you're a spoiled child in a roomful of toys, throwing a tantrum over the one toy you can't have."

He drew closer, looking down at her.

"Your refusal only drew my attention," he said huskily. "It wasn't the only reason. Something about you…" His gaze fell to her lips, and for a second she thought he might kiss her, right then and there on Main Street. She shivered, holding her breath as he said, "Take me up on the mountain."

Take me. Up on the mountain. She gulped.

"I can't," she breathed. "It's…locals only…"

"You can." His voice was so persuasive she felt

like she couldn't say no. In fact, she could barely remember what *no* meant.

Ruby took a deep breath. "Look, I'm sure you're a great skier, but—"

"Actually I'm not. I suck at skiing."

Her lips parted in astonishment, both at the assertion and that any arrogant man would admit to being bad at something. "Then why would you buy a house here?"

Ares looked at her. "There are other things I enjoy."

His voice was low, making her shiver in the cold night. He wasn't even touching her, but she felt electrified, half on fire. It had never felt like this with Braden, not once, not even when he'd kissed her. Even when he'd proposed to her, he'd never made her feel like this.

Run, her mother's voice warned inside her. *Run as far and fast as you can.*

Instead, as Ruby looked up at Ares beneath the diamond-sparkled winter moonlight, she heard herself say, "Do you have ski clothes?"

His cruel, sensual lips curved. "Of course."

She snorted. "But they're probably some expensive designer, aren't they? Brand new? In black?"

When he didn't deny it, Ruby shook her head. "I'll find you something else."

"What's wrong with my clothes?"

"No one can know I'm bringing you up on the mountain. They'd be furious. Think you can keep your mouth in check and be inconspicuous and quiet?"

He looked insulted. "I can be inconspicuous when I choose. In fact, I'm amazing at it."

She rolled her eyes. "Just do your best, okay? If anyone asks, you're my cousin's best friend from Coeur d'Alene. Come on." Motioning him to follow, she led him to her old, beat-up SUV parked on a side street. She opened the passenger-side door with a squeal of rusted metal. She had to wrench the handle just right to get it open.

Ares looked at the truck dubiously.

"Not scared of a little worn upholstery, are you?" she challenged.

"That truck is older than I am."

"How old are you?"

"Thirty-six."

"You're right. Get in."

Going to the driver's side, Ruby climbed in. He slid in beside her on the bench seat, then slammed the passenger door shut with a clang. It actually latched. She was impressed. Most people weren't strong enough to close it unless they knew the trick. She looked at him.

Ares looked out of place sitting on the worn bench seat in his elegant black cashmere coat and well-cut white shirt and black trousers. She hid a smile. If he was bothered by her old truck, just *wait* till he saw what she planned for him to wear up on the mountain. Her smile spread to a grin.

"Ruby?"

Starting the engine with a low roar, she glanced at him. "Yeah?"

Ares caught her gaze beneath the moonlight. "Thank you."

His dark eyes burned through her. Her grin faded. Looking away, she muttered, "It's no big deal." Glancing over her left shoulder, she twisted the steering wheel and pushed on the gas. "I'm just going to stop at my house and pick up some ski clothes for you."

"Whose are they? Your brother's? Your father's?" He paused. "Your lover's?"

"I don't have any of those things," she said, staring forward at the road. "My father deserted my mom before I was born. It's just my mom, my little sister and me."

"The same little sister who planned to seduce me?"

He sounded amused, but her cheeks burned. She could only imagine what he thought of Ivy. "Don't judge her. She should be in college, having fun. Instead, she spends most of her time in a sickroom. Our mom's been sick a long time. And Ivy doesn't even remember her father. He died a long time ago."

"You and your sister have different fathers?"

She looked at him fiercely. "So?"

He shrugged. "Sometimes I think fathers are overrated. My own was a piece of work."

Slightly mollified, she changed the subject. "Did you grow up in Greece? You don't really have an accent."

"I was born in Greece. But most of my life I've lived elsewhere. New York, mostly." For a moment, silence fell as she drove the truck down the thin sliver of highway going through the moonlit, snow-covered valley. Then he said, "In my experience, all fathers do well is pay the bills."

With a snort, Ruby shook her head. "My father never paid a single bill for us. Neither did Ivy's."

He frowned. "What about child support?"

"They found ways around it."

"But legally…"

Gripping the steering wheel, Ruby looked at the road. "It's complicated."

He turned away. "You don't have to explain."

She glanced at him, her mouth curving with humor. "What is that, reverse psychology?"

"No. I really don't need to know. I don't do complicated."

Ruby's lips parted. "What do you mean, you don't do complicated?"

"Just that."

"How do you have relationships, then?"

"When my relationships get complicated, they end. I don't do love, either. I don't even know what it is."

He sounded almost proud of that fact. "Is that why you broke up with your girlfriend?" Ruby asked. He gave her a sudden searching glance, and she ducked her head, embarrassed at her own curiosity. "Sorry. Everyone was talking about it at the club."

"No. Poppy didn't need me to love her. That was one of her best qualities. But her debut film didn't do as well as she hoped at the festival. She wanted me to fly her to the Himalayas on some mystical experience to seek redemption. I declined. She left. End of story."

Ruby turned her truck off the highway.

"Where are you going?"

"Star Valley's expensive. Most of the people who work there can't afford to live there. I live in Sawtooth."

"How far?"

"About twenty minutes more." Turning her truck onto a rough mountain road, she glanced at him. "I heard you have a private jet."

"I have a few." His voice wasn't boastful, just factual.

Her eyes went wide. "A few jets! What's that even like?"

He shrugged. "They get me where I need to go."

In Ruby's one flying experience, traveling to Portland to visit an old high school friend, she'd been stuck in a middle seat in economy, between two oversize men who took her armrests and invaded her space. The flight had arrived an hour late, and her suitcase had arrived twelve hours after that.

Thinking of what it might be like to have one's own private fleet, she shook her head, a little awed in spite of herself. "I can't even imagine."

"It's no big deal."

"It must be hell." Tilting her head, she gave him

a cheerful grin. "Your friends must be always hitting you up for rides. Nagging and begging all the time."

The corners of his lips curved upward. "Actually, they don't. Most of them have planes of their own."

That brought her up short.

"Oh," she said faintly. As she changed gears, her old truck rattled and coughed smoke behind them. "I live just up here."

Ares turned to look out the window, and unwillingly, her eyes lingered on his silhouette. The hard line of his jaw, the curve of his lips. He was so handsome, she thought. So masculine. So powerful. So everything she was not.

Then, following the direction of his gaze, she saw her neighborhood with fresh eyes. The trailer park was small, tidy and well maintained. Ruby's neighbors were kind and hardworking, but the trailers looked old and plain, with snow piled haphazardly on the road. The flowers that made the street so beautiful in summer were nowhere to be seen in winter. And her neighbors' cars, like her own, had all seen better days.

As she parked in front of her own family's single-wide mobile home, she saw how careworn it had become. But good people lived in this neighborhood. Good people who worked hard. Telling herself she had nothing to be ashamed of, she put her truck into park and turned off the engine. "Would you like to come in?"

Ares's darkly handsome, chiseled face held no expression. "To meet your sick mother and the little sister who was planning to trap me into marriage?"

"Right. You don't do complicated." She tried to keep her voice light, even as her cheeks burned. "I'll be right back."

Closing the door solidly behind her, Ruby went into her home. The living room was dark. "Ivy? Mom?"

"I'm in here," her mother's voice called weakly.

Ruby hurried into her mother's small bedroom and found Bonnie propped up in bed, a small television blaring from an opposite shelf. Pill bottles were on her nightstand table, along with an untouched plate of food.

"Mom! You didn't eat!"

"I wasn't…hungry," her mother said apologetically. Her voice was small, and she paused to take breaths sometimes between words. "Why are you…here?"

"I got out of work early, so I'm going up on the mountain for Renegade Night."

Her mother beamed at her, her kind blue eyes shining.

Ruby hesitated. "I'm, um, bringing someone. A man I just met." She bit her lip, but she wasn't used to hiding things from her mother, so she finished reluctantly, "That Greek guy who bought the thirty-million-dollar house."

The smile slid from Bonnie's wasted face. "No." She shook her head weakly. "Rich men…cannot love…"

"Don't worry," Ruby said quickly. "It's not like that. We're not on a date. He just helped me get the night off, so I'm returning the favor by bringing him on the mountain. I'm sure I'll never see him again." Lowering her head, she kissed her mother's forehead. Drawing back with a frown, she touched Bonnie's forehead with her hand. "You feel cold."

"I'm fine. Ivy said…be home soon."

"She called you?"

"She…was here. Changed to…jeans. Out with friends. Pizza."

Ruby hoped that was true, and that Ivy wasn't trying to get into some other club downtown. But if she'd changed into jeans, that was unlikely. And she knew Ivy wouldn't be on the mountain. She hated winter sports with a passion. "I could stay with you."

"Go," Bonnie said firmly. "You deserve…fun. You always take care…of us." She took a rasping breath. "Go."

"All right," Ruby said reluctantly. She squeezed her mother's hand and smiled. "When I get back tonight, I'll hopefully have funny stories to share. I love you, Mom."

"Love…you…"

Ruby hurried down the hall to the oversize closet, where she stored all the interesting vintage clothes she'd collected over the years, in dreams of someday starting her own business. Now, let's see, where had she put it? Digging through boxes, she finally found what she was looking for and grinned. She could hardly wait to see Ares's face.

CHAPTER THREE

SCATTERING SNOW AS he twisted his snowboard to a stop halfway down the mountain, Ares straightened, looking back.

The night was clear and dark with stars. He could see his breath in the cold air, illuminated by moonlight and the slow trail of fire-lit torches of skiers zigzagging single file down the mountain. He'd never seen anything so beautiful.

Or maybe he had.

Ruby came to an abrupt stop next to him on her snowboard, pelting him with a wave of snow. Her face was indescribably beautiful as she laughed merrily, her cheeks pink with cold, her eyes sparkling bright.

"For a man who claimed to suck at skiing," she observed, "you're pretty good."

"This is snowboarding. I never claimed to suck at snowboarding."

"Flying down the hill like that, I thought you'd break your neck. No doubt causing anguish to starlets and lingerie models everywhere," she added drily.

He grinned. "Don't forget the swimsuit models."

Her trash talk reassured him. He knew if she'd been underwhelmed by his snowboarding skills, she would have instead been patronizingly kind. He was relieved, since he'd nearly broken his damn neck trying to stay ahead of her.

Ares looked back at the torchlit parade. "I've never seen anything like this."

"I'm happy to be here." Looking at him, she said softly, "Thank you, Ares."

Hearing her low, melodic voice speak his name, he felt a strange twist in his heart. Was it her beauty? Was it the winter fantasy around him, the sense that he was a million miles away from his real life?

It was excitement, he told himself. Excitement and lust. And triumph. He was winning her over. She would soon be his.

Ruby gave him a sudden cheerful grin. "No one even recognized you."

Wryly, he glanced down at his vintage 1980s one-piece ski suit, bright blue with white and red racing stripes. He'd almost refused to wear it when she'd given it to him. Then he'd realized it was a test of sorts, and had taken it without complaint, along with the antiquated snowboard equipment, old goggles and a dark beanie hat from the resort's lost-and-found bin.

"Perfect," she'd said when he'd come out of the dressing room, her eyes twinkling with glee. "You'll fit right in."

And somewhat to his surprise, he had. The other ski instructors participating in Renegade Night were mostly in their twenties, both men and women, all of them fit and reckless. Even with Ares's height and broad physique, no one had looked at him twice. Not with two Olympic athletes joining them, Star Valley locals who'd won medals in ski jumping and downhill skiing. And also some famous hockey player, apparently. They were the local heroes. No one had looked twice at Ares in his thick goggles.

It was disconcerting. But also strangely liberating.

Anonymity meant privacy. It meant freedom. That kind of invisibility was exhilarating and new.

Even as a boy in Greece, Ares had been constantly under a microscope, the only child of Aristedes and Thalia Kourakis, the glamorous, fabulously wealthy Greek society couple. His mother was famous for her beauty, his father for his ruth-less power, and both of them for their tempestu-ous marriage, a five-year battle that had ended in a ten-year divorce.

And if they were merciless to each other, they'd been even more so to their only son. They'd used him as a pawn, first in the marriage, then in their divorce, in the court of public opinion. Ares had been recognized, and fawned over, wherever he went, if not for his appearance, then for his fam-ily's wealth and name.

Appearance was what mattered. His parents had taught him that well, spending almost no time with him, leaving him in the care of nannies as they tried to outdo each other by buying him ridiculous gifts. The gifts always came with strings. Like on Ares's ninth birthday, when his father had bought him a Brazilian aerospace company. As Ares had blinked in confusion—he'd dreamed of a puppy—his father had added casually, "And in return for this amazing gift, I expect you to report on the ac-tivities of that whore you call a mother."

Now, as Ares felt the ice-cold wind of the Idaho mountain whip against his face, he realized he'd never had the chance to cast off his name and everything that came with it—fame, power, yes, but also darkness.

He felt strangely free. Strangely alive.

"Why are you just standing there? Don't tell me you're already tired," Ruby said gleefully.

Ares looked at the beautiful, unexpected woman beside him in the snow. Her cloud of dark hair tumbled beneath her pink hat, knit with a red flower. Behind her, he saw the distant torches of the last skiers, as lovely and mysterious as fairy lights.

He wasn't tired. At all.

He wanted to kiss her.

He wanted to do far more than kiss her.

Looking at him, Ruby's expression changed. Her smile slid away. She looked almost...afraid.

"Come on." Turning on her snowboard, she took off down the hill. She was reckless, jumping moguls. She was a force of nature. Unstoppable.

Ares watched her. He'd possessed many women in his life. He'd taken them as his due. But for the first time, he'd met one who didn't seem overly impressed either by his money or his appearance. She accepted him—or not—only for himself. For his actions. For his words. For his skills.

He could hardly wait to win her into his bed.

Chasing her, Ares turned the snowboard down and flew.

She reached the bottom of the mountain first. A roaring bonfire crackled in the middle of a snowy field, next to an icy creek. Around it, young people who'd already finished skiing laughed together, holding steaming mugs.

Ares unlatched his snowboard. Lifting his goggles to his ski cap, he straightened, stepping out in the snow in his borrowed boots. Someone he didn't know handed him a copper mug.

"Here, man. This'll warm you up."

Pulling off his gloves, Ares stuffed them in his pockets and took the mug. "Thanks."

"I'm Gus." The red-haired man, who had a lumberjack beard, did a double take. "Nice snowsuit."

Ares scowled, suspecting mockery. But the other man's eyes were sincere. So he said, "Thank you."

"Ruby picked that out for you, right? You're her friend's cousin or something from up north?"

"Hmm," Ares said noncommittally. Sniffing cinnamon and clove, he took a tentative sip from the copper mug. He tasted mulled wine, hot and infused with spices. Sighing in pleasure, he took a bigger gulp.

"Right," Gus said. "That girl has mad skills tracking down vintage stuff. I keep telling her she needs to start that business. All she needs to do is apply for a loan, but she just won't."

"A business?" Ares's eyebrows lifted. He looked down at his outrageous ski suit. "You think people would actually buy outfits like this? On purpose?"

"Oh, yeah, man. Look around."

He did, and he saw that most of the young people were indeed dressed in funky, offbeat outfits as outlandish as his own.

"Designer gear is for talentless hacks trying to buy their way into the sport." The red-haired man considered. "Your suit is cool."

Ares's gaze fell on Ruby, who was standing on the other side of the bonfire. A broad-shouldered man was talking to her earnestly. "Who's that with her now?"

The young man nodded toward them. "You know Braden Lassiter is her ex, right? They were engaged until he up and left for the National Hockey League. He plays for New York."

Ares's eyes narrowed. "New York?" He strained to remember anything he'd heard about Braden Lassiter, but he didn't follow ice hockey. But he didn't like seeing him talking to Ruby. *Leaning* toward her. "They were engaged?"

"High school sweethearts. Too bad they broke up. If they had a baby, man, that kid would kill it on the slopes, probably win every gold medal."

Ares stared at them. A moment ago, flying down the mountain, he'd felt exhilarated, even euphoric. Now he felt ice in his solar plexus. What was it? Irritation? Possessiveness? It couldn't be jealousy. He didn't *do* jealousy.

Finishing his drink, Ares handed the mug back. "Thanks again."

At least he wasn't the only one who was annoyed. As he walked toward Ruby, he saw Braden Lassiter walking away from her with a scowl on his face. The man paused to stare suspiciously as Ares approached her.

Turning, Ruby saw him. "There you are."

Ares jerked his chin toward the departing hockey player. "Was he bothering you?"

"Braden?" She rolled her eyes. "His team was playing in Vancouver and he had a free day, so he dropped in for Renegade Night. So of course the second he sees me with someone, he's suddenly Mr. Twenty Questions, like he thinks he still has some claim over me."

"You were engaged?"

"Did Gus tell you?" A strange expression crossed

her face. "It was a million years ago. When he became an instant millionaire, he disappeared."

"The bastard."

"It was a good reminder of what money does to men's hearts."

The snow crunched beneath his feet. "And what is that?"

She looked up at him with big, dark eyes that gleamed against the bonfire's flickering red light. "It makes them selfish. And cold."

Ares immediately knew the accusation didn't only include Braden Lassiter. "Or maybe," he said quietly, "we were always that way from the start, and money just gave us more opportunity."

She stared at him for a long moment by the crackling fire. Then she sighed, watching as sparks flew up into the dark, cold, starlit sky. "I wish there was no such thing as money."

Close together in front of the bonfire, he could feel the warmth of the flames against his body. But it was nothing compared to the heat he felt inside as he looked down at her.

"I'm glad there is," he said. "Because it's why I'm here with you right now."

Her lips parted. "I didn't bring you here for money!"

"I know. But you'd still be working at the bar." Gently, he stroked down her cheek to caress her lower lip with the tip of his thumb. "I couldn't have blackmailed you into bringing me here."

He heard her catch her breath, felt her tremble beneath his touch. So she felt it, too, then. *She felt it, too.*

"You didn't exactly…blackmail me."

Ares looked down at her lovely face, lit up by the firelight. "I didn't?"

"No," she admitted, then took a deep breath. "Maybe," she whispered, "you're different, too…"

Burning wood crackled in the bonfire as they looked at each other. He heard the burble of the creek, the soft drop of snow falling from pine trees, the wind blowing through the valley.

The fire glowed in her expressive dark eyes, even as the other side of her dark hair was laced silver by moonlight. Silver and gold, he thought. Why did Ruby continually remind him of a princess from a fairy tale? A sexy fairy tale that ended with them naked in each other's arms. She obliterated his every thought except need…

Ares cupped both sides of her face, beneath her jawline. Her skin, chilled by the cold air, warmed beneath his hands. He felt her tremble as her delectable, cherry-red lips parted, as if in invitation.

Lowering his mouth to hers, he kissed her.

Sweet, so sweet. Her lips were satin soft, and tasted like sugar. They tasted like heaven. He felt her shiver. Her lips caused a delicious fire to roar though him, building higher and higher, until his body was blazing from within.

Then, reaching her hands around his shoulders, she started to kiss him back.

The fire inside him exploded. With a low growl, he pulled her hard against him, forgetting all the others milling around them, forgetting everything else in the world but the taste of her sweet lips and feel of her curvaceous body against his.

As if from a distance, he heard the low shouts, lazy applause, yelled encouragements and commentary from the people around them.

"Get a room," someone hooted.

"I thought he was her cousin," someone else said.

"Who is he?"

"Oh, my God, is that…Ares Kourakis?"

The last words broke the spell, and as a branch snapped loudly in the fire, he felt Ruby stiffen in his arms. But he wouldn't release her.

Tangling his hands in her hair, Ares murmured, "Let's get out of here. Come home with me."

Her face looked stricken, almost dazed, as she glanced around at her friends. Licking her lips, she whispered, "I—I shouldn't."

"Just for one drink."

"I told you. I don't drink."

He grasped at straws. "We haven't eaten anything all night. You must be hungry. Let me make you dinner."

"You cook?"

Growing up with a house full of servants, Ares had never cooked in his life. But he wasn't going to admit that now. "I'll make you something amazing."

The edges of her lips curved upward. "How amazing?"

He looked her straight in the eye. "The best you've ever had."

Her eyes widened at his obvious implication. Glancing right and left self-consciously, she said in a low voice, "I can't."

His dark eyebrows lifted. "I took you for the kind of girl who doesn't care what other people think. Only about her own pleasure."

She choked a laugh. "What made you think that?"

He held her gaze. "When was the last time you put yourself first?"

"Tonight. Being here with you."

"And before that?"

She paused. "It's been a while."

Pulling her more tightly into his arms, he looked down at her, relishing the feel of her against him in the cold night. "You can have anything you desire." He stroked his fingertips slowly against her cheek. "All you have to do is say yes."

Ruby's pink cheeks turned redder still. She said unsteadily, "You're just saying that trying to get what *you* want."

"Of course I am," he said frankly. "I want you, Ruby. I haven't tried to hide it. Or the fact that I'm selfish and ruthless…"

Lowering his head to hers, he kissed her until she was left shivering in his arms and clinging to him for balance.

"Stop," she breathed when he pulled away, again to more hooting from her friends. "I'll come."

Triumph filled him. "You will?"

She looked at him helplessly. "For dinner. Nothing more."

But that was a lie, and he knew it. The way she'd kissed him, she had to know full well that food would barely be an appetizer on their sensual menu. But if her pride needed that ridiculous self-deception, he'd be the last man to argue the point.

As she gathered her gloves and said a quiet thank-you to her friends, he watched her hungrily. He could still feel her mouth against his. Still taste her lips. Waiting was agony. Every moment they weren't naked felt like eternity.

Tucking both their snowboards under his arm, Ares followed her down the short path to the quiet, snowy lot where her beat-up truck was parked. She hesitated, giving an unsteady laugh as she looked back at him.

"I don't think I can drive." She lifted a hand to her forehead. "I feel a little wobbly. It's been a long day. Maybe I have low blood sugar. I don't know what's wrong with me."

"I'll drive."

"You were drinking."

He gave a low laugh. "Two sips of scotch, half a beer, and a mug of mulled wine, over four hours."

"My truck can be tricky—"

He took her keys. "I've got it." Unlocking the back, he tossed in the snowboards. He opened her door and helped her climb onto the bench seat, next to a canvas duffel bag filled with their regular clothes. Touching her hand, he felt her tremble. Or was he the one trembling?

He stomped on the thought. It was ridiculous.

Ruby Prescott was just another woman. A woman like any other. Once he possessed her, once the attraction was consummated, he would be satisfied. He could leave for Sydney tomorrow and not give her another thought.

Ruby was different from the rest, yes.

But not *that* different.

Ruby had never believed in fairy tales. She couldn't. Not growing up as she had.

Her mother was the kindest, best person on the planet. Bonnie always saw the best in people and believed good things were just around the corner. She believed if you worked hard, had faith in your dreams and took care of others, you would be happy.

Her mother had been wrong.

In spite of being so good, in spite of being so kind, Bonnie had suffered bad luck and misfortune. Her parents, Ruby's grandparents, had died before Bonnie was nineteen, leaving little savings.

Unwilling to leave her hometown, she'd become a waitress the summer after high school. She was trying to save for college when she was swept off her feet by a resort guest, a handsome millionaire visiting from Buenos Aires. Bonnie had thought it was true love, just like she'd always dreamed of. But when she became pregnant with Ruby, instead of being delighted and proposing marriage as Bonnie had hoped, the man had screamed in her face, tossed a few hundred-dollar bills in her face for an abortion and left the country, never to return.

Bonnie had moved into a trailer with cheap rent, temporarily she'd thought, trying to raise her baby daughter on minimum-wage jobs, still hoping she could improve their situation. Instead, when Ruby was five, her mother had fallen in love with another wealthy hotel guest, this one a Texas oilman ten years Bonnie's senior, whom she hoped might be a good father to Ruby.

Over the course of an entire winter of visits, he'd told Bonnie he loved her. He hadn't always wanted to use a condom, and believing they'd soon be married, she'd reluctantly acquiesced. But when summer came and she discovered she was pregnant, he wouldn't marry her. "I'm married to my comp'ny, darlin'," he'd said with a smile, in his charming cowboy drawl. And as for child support, he'd taken her in his arms and tenderly asked her not to make any legal claim. "Just wait a little while. Till this next oil field pans out. Then I'll take care of you and that lil' baby, don't you worry."

But he never did. He just stopped coming to Star Valley, and ignored Bonnie's increasingly frantic messages. Before Ivy was even born, oil prices suddenly collapsed, and his overextended company was forced into bankruptcy. Unable to face the total loss, he drove his car into a telephone pole, in a fiery death the coroner obligingly marked "accident."

After that, Bonnie had learned her lesson. She'd told her daughters again and again never to trust anything a rich man might tell them.

And look what good it had done, Ruby thought. Ivy still dreamed of hooking a rich husband. And Ruby herself, as a foolish eighteen-year-old, had nearly married Braden, who'd abandoned her the second the ink on his NHL contract was dry.

Fairy tales weren't real. Romantic dreams were poison. Men who seemed like handsome princes were just lying, trying to lure sensible young women into love—and doom.

What had love ever done for her mother except

destroy her ability to follow her own dreams, leaving her heartbroken and poor?

What had it done for Ruby other than leaving her alone and humiliated at the altar?

Ruby was just relieved that Braden had left her when he had. When their love was still innocent. Before they'd married, or worse, had a child. But she had no intention of ever trusting a rich, ruthless man ever again.

Then, tonight, Ares had kissed her.

It was the kiss Ruby had dreamed about, even while telling herself that romantic dreams were lies. The kiss she'd been waiting for all her life.

He'd held her tightly beside the flames of the bonfire, beneath the cold, bright stars, and when his lips had touched hers, she'd forgotten all her sensible plans and promises.

There was only this.

Only him.

Now Ruby glanced at him out of the corner of her eye as he drove her old truck down the snowy road. Her gaze lingered on his sensual lips, and she felt her own tingle in memory of his embrace.

Her eyes traced unwillingly over his strong arms, as he changed gears; over his strong thighs, as he pressed on the gas. She'd never let anyone drive her truck before, but she'd had no choice tonight, because her own knees felt so weak, for reasons that she knew had nothing to do with hunger or snowboarding.

Ares was right. She was hungry. After so many years being strong for everyone else, she felt like she'd been starving for years, on a treadmill of unending work. There'd been no color. No joy.

I took you for the kind of girl who doesn't care what other people think. Only about her own pleasure.

A shiver racked Ruby's body. But she couldn't let herself be tempted. He'd already told her outright that he was selfish and ruthless. He didn't do complicated. Why would she be foolish enough to believe any love affair between them, even a one-night stand, could end any way but badly?

And yet…

Staring at him, her heart was pounding. She felt danger. Pleasure. Excitement. In this moment, she couldn't think straight. All she could do was feel.

She was tempted. Even knowing herself for a fool. *She wanted him.* His kiss had overwhelmed her senses. Her toes still hadn't uncurled in her boots.

Ares glanced at her. His black eyes glinted in

the darkness, and heat flooded her body. Then he turned away as he steered the truck onto a small private road, and she exhaled.

All right, so maybe she'd become a modern-day spinster, a twenty-four-year-old virgin who worked too much and, as her little sister had pointed out, who had apparently given up on her dreams. But if Ruby truly wanted to change that, if she wanted to take her first lover, it would be better to proposition Monty or even Paul Vence himself rather than let herself be seduced by the selfish, arrogant Greek billionaire everyone else wanted. Whom even her baby sister had wanted.

As if on cue, Ruby heard her phone ringing from her canvas duffel bag. Digging through neatly folded clothes, she looked at it and saw Ivy's number. Guilt rushed through her. After the way she'd prevented Ivy from sleeping with Ares, the word *hypocrite* didn't even seem large enough to describe how her sister would see Ruby's actions right now. She pressed the button to decline the call.

"Everything all right?"

Ares's voice was sensual, low, and it did crazy things to her insides. "Everything's fine." Biting her lip, she took a deep breath and said in a rush,

"But I think I changed my mind about dinner and I should just go home—"

His hands tightened on the steering wheel. "Is that what you want?"

"Yes—it is—"

Ares stopped the truck abruptly in the middle of the dark, empty road. Turning off the engine, he looked at her.

"You're lying." His hot dark gaze pierced her from across the worn bench seat. "There's no way you want to go home. Not after the way you kissed me."

She shrugged, trying desperately to play it cool. "I guess the kiss wasn't totally bad…"

"Bad?" He looked incredulous.

"…but it was just a kiss." She was proud of the way her voice held steady, as if his embrace beneath the winter sky hadn't twisted her body inside out and turned her heart upside down, leaving her weak and yearning.

"We both know it was more." His voice held an edge. "You felt it. I felt it."

"I don't know what you're talking about."

He looked astonished, then angry. Moving across the truck's bench seat, he grabbed her by the shoulders, looking down at her fiercely. "Before I met you, I felt bored by everything and everyone. But now there's one thing I can't stop thinking about. One thing I have to have. At any price."

Ruby's heart was pounding. He was saying everything that she felt, deep in her soul. Trembling, she choked out, "I thought you didn't do complicated..."

"This isn't complicated. It's simple. I want you to come home with me tonight. And I know you feel the same. Why are you trying to deny it?"

As their eyes locked, her phone started to ring from her bag. Glancing down, she saw it was Ivy again. Ruby looked from the phone to him, torn between reason and desire.

I know you feel the same. Why are you trying to deny it?

She took a deep breath. From the moment she'd first seen him in the nightclub, she'd wanted him. She'd tried to pretend otherwise. Because fairy tales didn't come true, and there could be no bigger fairy tale than a handsome billionaire flying into a small mountain town and choosing a nobody like Ruby over every other woman in the world.

A rich man only wanted things he couldn't have. Ruby knew this. Once possessed, a prize no longer had value. If she let him seduce her, Ares would soon look for new worlds—new women—to conquer.

And if she was wrong? If their affair lasted longer than a night?

That could be even worse. Because falling in love with a man like Ares, depending on him, could destroy her life, just as it had her mother's.

And yet…

As she felt his hand move slowly up her arm, every nerve in her body sang with longing. She closed her eyes, holding her breath, hanging off the edge of the cliff.

Her phone started ringing yet again. With a single sharp movement, Ruby abruptly turned it off.

Holding her breath, she opened her eyes.

"Just dinner," she whispered.

Ares's sensual lips curved. Something deeper and more primal than satisfaction simmered in his dark eyes. Starting the truck again, he drove up the private road, pressing down hard on the gas, going as fast as the engine would allow.

CHAPTER FOUR

JUST DINNER.

Even as Ruby spoke the words, she knew she was playing with fire. Every moment she spent with Ares she was getting in deeper. It would be too easy to be seduced by him. Even knowing that it could only lead to heartbreak.

But she couldn't go back home. Not yet. For too long, she'd lived only to take care of her family, until she'd forgotten what it felt like to do anything but work. Most of the emotions she'd known for the last year had been bad ones. The worsening of her mother's illness. Her sister's petulant anger. Long, painful battles with insurance companies and bill collectors.

Now she watched Ares drive faster and faster down the one-lane forest road, as if being chased by a hurricane. As if the powerful, handsome billionaire thought his life would be worth nothing unless he got Ruby to his expensive house—now.

There's one thing I can't stop thinking about. One thing I have to have. At any price.

Ruby shivered. Being desired in such a way was new to her. It was almost impossible to resist. But she would.

I'll just stay an hour, she told herself desperately. *Just a little while. Dinner, and maybe a kiss. Maybe a few kisses.* She wouldn't let it go further.

For one short evening, she needed to forget her real life. She needed to feel pleasure. She needed to feel *alive.*

Then she would go back to her real life with a memory she could treasure, of one night when she'd been romanced, pursued, cherished by a handsome prince.

After stopping at an electronic gate, Ares punched in a code. The gate swung open. They drove past a few cottages, some distance from the main house.

"Who lives there?"

"The house's caretaker and housekeeper. My bodyguard. My driver."

His voice was husky. Shivering, Ruby asked no more questions. She saw the main house looming up ahead, the lit windows shining gold in the darkness. The house was made of rock and wood, enormous and brand-new.

The huge driveway had been carefully cleared of snow. Ares parked her truck directly in front of the house and helped her out.

At the front door, he punched in another security code. He held the door open for her courteously, even as his eyes devoured her as she walked past him into the foyer.

Inside, the house had changed since she'd been on the cleaning crew. Back then, it had been staged to appeal to the most potential buyers with colorful walls and comfortable sofas. That was all gone. Now the elegant furnishings were Spartan and spare, and everything was black-and-white.

Stopping in the mudroom, a room that existed for the purpose of removing wet ski clothes, they pulled off their boots. She took off her ski jacket, then hesitated.

He touched the zipper of her ski overalls. "Need help?"

Ruby's cheeks instantly flooded with heat as she quickly turned away. "No…"

"Suit yourself." He unzipped his colorful 1980s-era snowsuit, peeling it off his body and stepping out of it without the slightest self-consciousness. Ruby's eyes widened as she glanced at his hard-muscled bare chest, naked above his low-slung black trousers. When he caught her looking, he gave her a sensual, heavy-lidded smile that caused prickles to spin through her.

Turning quickly to the duffel bag she'd brought from the truck, she pulled out his black cashmere coat, his shirt and shoes. "Um. Here's your stuff."

"Thanks." But he didn't move to take them from the mudroom bench. He didn't try to hide his naked chest or turn away. He didn't even seem embarrassed. And why should he be? His muscular body was magnificent, hard-bodied and strong. In spite of her best efforts, her fascinated gaze unwillingly followed the trail of dark hair leading down his flat belly like an arrow, disappearing beneath the black waistband.

He came closer.

"Take these off." Gently tugging on the elasticized suspenders of her ski overalls, he said softly, "You wouldn't want to drip water and make my poor housekeeper have to re-wax the floors, would you?"

His voice was teasing, but she took it seriously. Waxing floors was a pain.

"No." She sighed, and unzipped her ski pants and stepped out of them, leaving them neatly folded on the duffel bag. Beneath, she was wearing the typical underlayer she always kept in her locker at the mountain—a long-sleeved black shirt and black leggings, both of which fit her like a glove.

Ares slowly looked over her body. She heard the soft whistle of his breath through his teeth. She knocked him off kilter as well, she realized. Ruby didn't know how it was possible. But she did.

"Just dinner," she said aloud.

"Of course," he murmured, a wicked gleam in his eye. "Come with me."

Taking her hand, he led her down the hallway to an enormous kitchen. When he turned on the light, she saw gleaming white marble with luxurious appliances. Everything was immaculate. There wasn't so much as a smudge on the fridge.

"Your housekeeper does a good job," she said.

"It looks nice, doesn't it?" He looked around, then grinned. "This is actually my first time in the kitchen."

"What? I thought you said you knew how to cook!"

Ares gave her a boyishly guilty grin. "I, um, do know how to cook a few things. Cereal. Sandwiches."

She gave a low laugh. "That's what I thought."

"It's not my fault. I was raised with servants."

"That's a very sad story," she said ironically, then gave him a cheerful grin. "On the other hand, it's nice to finally find someone who's as bad a cook as I am."

His eyebrows lifted. "You can't cook?"

"Only if it comes in a box, like macaroni and cheese. Ivy was always the cook of the family."

"Hmm. Well, let's see what the housekeeper has stocked in here." Opening the fridge, he perused the contents and said triumphantly, "I'm going to blow your mind."

Five minutes later, he served Ruby a sandwich of hand-carved chicken served on a freshly baked baguette, with crisp lettuce, juicy tomato and a variety of exquisite cheeses imported from England and Denmark.

Carrying their plates, they went into the enormous main room, with its two-story wall of windows revealing the view of the biggest ski mountain, Mt. Chaldie, beneath the moonlight. Nearby, a white-brick fireplace stretched to the ceiling. Ares flicked on a switch, and a gas fire, set in an architectural arrangement of black pebbles, came roaring to life.

Throughout the house, the decor was stark. An elegant upright white sectional sofa was positioned in front of the fire over a fluffy white rug and black wood floors. The rug looked more comfortable to sit on than the hard sofa, so Ruby sat down on it in front of the fire, still holding her plate.

Setting his own plate on the wide white hearth, he went to a small wet bar. "What will you have to drink?"

"A club soda," Ruby said primly.

"You're kidding."

"Why would I be?"

He glanced back at her. "Why don't you drink?"

Ruby shrugged. "It's expensive and I'm too busy."

"Too busy for fun?"

"I tried a beer once. I didn't like it."

"Ever try champagne?"

"No," she admitted.

His dark eyes challenged her. "Want to?"

She paused, biting her lip as she considered. "Would I like it?"

"Try it." Opening the wine fridge, he pulled out a champagne bottle. She saw the label and gasped. It was the kind of superluxurious, superrare brand that the Atlas Club sold only a few times a year, usually when the McFallon and Company convention was in town, or maybe when some sheikh or

Russian zillionaire wanted to prove that he was the richest fool on the planet.

"You're crazy," she said. "That bottle is worth more than my truck."

He snorted. "*Anything* is worth more than your truck."

"What if I don't like it?"

"You will."

"You should just give me the cheap kind. I won't know the difference."

"I'm not giving you the cheap kind of anything." He popped the cork.

Ruby stretched out on the fluffy white rug, warming her feet by the fire. Coming to sit on the rug beside her, he handed her a champagne glass, then clinked it with his own.

"To Renegade Night," he whispered, and drank deeply.

Watching him, she hesitantly took a sip of champagne. It was cool and sweet and she felt the bubbles all the way to her toes.

"Do you like it?"

"Yes," she said honestly.

"The bouquet goes well with the sandwich." She wondered if he was teasing. At his grin, she decided he was.

She took a bite of her sandwich, then sighed with pleasure. "You're right. You *can* cook."

"I told you," he said smugly.

She scarfed down most of her sandwich before she realized that he hadn't touched his. She frowned. "Why aren't you eating?"

He set down his glass. His eyes met hers, and all the world seemed to hold its breath.

"That's not what I'm hungry for," he said in a low voice.

He took the champagne glass from her hand, then her plate, moving them to the stone hearth next to his.

Leaning forward on the thick white rug, Ares pulled her against his body. She could feel the heat radiating off his naked chest and powerful arms, hotter than the fire.

Slowly, he lowered his head to hers and scorched her lips with his hard, hungry kiss. His mouth plundered hers, drawing her into a blaze she could not resist.

His hands moved slowly down her body, over the thin fabric of her knit shirt and leggings. Her skin tingled beneath his touch, and the nerves of her body electrified from her hair to her toes. Her breasts became heavy, the nipples aching and hard.

Without realizing it, she reached her arms around his shoulders, clutching him closer. She gave a low gasp as she felt the warmth and strength of his naked back, his skin smooth satin over hard muscle.

Lowering her back against the thick white rug in front of the fire, he kissed slowly down her throat. She tilted back her head, her dark hair tumbling around her in waves, eyes closed as she felt his hands running roughly over her body, beneath her shirt, over her naked belly. His fingertips felt delicious against her skin, caressing her, commanding her. All her earlier promises to herself were lost and forgotten.

For long moments, he kissed her, until their lips were both bruised, their bodies straining for each other. Until even surrender was long behind her and she was kissing him back with a hunger that met his own.

Rising to his feet, Ares lifted her in his strong arms, holding her against his chest as if she weighed nothing. He carried her down his dark hall into an enormous shadowy bedroom and switched on the fire in the stark fireplace. The massive bed was illuminated in a pool of moonlight that shone in from the window like a spotlight.

She desperately tried to remember why she couldn't let this happen. But at this moment, being in his arms seemed like everything she'd ever wanted. She could no more resist him than she could resist life itself.

Maybe she'd been wrong all this time, she thought in a daze. Maybe fairy tales really could come true...

Letting her smaller body slide down against his, he set her down on her feet. She felt the hardness of his desire for her.

He drew her arms over her head, pulling off her long-sleeved shirt. As if from a distance, she watched it fall to the floor, her heart pounding. He towered over her, so powerful and certain, as his hands caressed down her back to unhook the clasp of her bra. She heard his low hiss of appreciation as her breasts sprung free and her bra fell to the floor. Awed, he cupped one of her breasts in his hand.

"So beautiful," he whispered. "I've been wanting to do this all night."

Lowering his head, he pulled her taut red nipple into his wet, hot mouth.

Pleasure spiraled through her, making her gasp as he suckled her. Caressing her breasts with his hands, he pulled away, kneeling before her. His large hands moved to her waist, then her hips as he slowly pulled off her black leggings, peeling the flimsy fabric down her thighs, to her knees, to her ankles. He lifted one of her feet, then the other, and the leggings disappeared completely, leaving her standing before him wearing only her white cotton panties. Still on his knees, he briefly pressed his head against her belly, closing his eyes.

Then he exhaled, running his hands up her half-naked backside. Moving his head, he ran the scratchy edge of his jaw against her hip, sliding down toward the crux between her legs, along the edge of her underwear. Sensation rushed through her. She watched the flickering firelight against his back, felt the bedroom's soft rug between her toes. She felt the heat of his breath against her skin.

After pulling her panties to the floor, he slowly lowered his head between her thighs.

And he tasted her.

Gripping his shoulders, she gave a loud gasp as spirals of pleasure twisted through her. As the wet roughness of his tongue slowly worked against her most sensitive core, the pleasure was too much, spinning out of control. She knew she should pull him away, make him stop, but not now...not yet!

Her head fell back in ecstasy, long hair tumbling down her shoulders as she held her breath. Her nipples were tight, her whole body tense, coiling with hot, building need.

"Sweet," he whispered against her skin. "So sweet."

Gently, he pushed her back on the bed. Eyes squeezed shut, she heard him remove the remainder of his clothes. She felt the mattress shift beneath her, and then the weight of his hard-muscled body naked over hers. She felt the hard length of him pressing against her thigh. She was lost. Lost.

He slowly moved down the length of her, kissing and caressing her skin. Then he lowered his head back between her legs.

Her shaking hands held the comforter beneath her tightly as he licked her. Spreading her wide, he pushed the tip of his tongue a single inch inside her. She was overwhelmed by intense pleasure buffeting her like hurricane-force winds. Using his lips and tongue, he drew her gently into the deep, warm pleasure of his mouth. It was too much. Her fingers twisted in his short dark hair, but he would not move away. He would not release her. A low cry built in the back of her throat as he held her down, encouraging her to surrender to the pleasure.

She exploded in a cry she didn't recognize as her own, as she soared and shattered into a thousand chiming prisms of her body and soul.

With a growl, he rose on the bed, leaning to take a condom from his nightstand. Drawing it down in a single skilled movement over the huge, hard erection jutting from his body, he positioned himself between her legs.

Distracted from the aftershocks of her climax, she felt the hot slide of his muscular body against hers as he spread her legs wide and pushed deep inside her.

Pain shot through her. She gasped, gripping her nails into his shoulders.

He froze, his face a picture of shock. "You were…a virgin?"

She nodded, then closed her eyes, turning her head away.

"How could you be?" His voice was low, almost angry.

How could she explain? That she'd been waiting for true love, for a knight in shining armor to sweep her off her feet? That even at eighteen, when she'd agreed to marry Braden, part of her had known he wouldn't be that man?

"Ruby."

Reluctantly, she looked up at him. Ares's grimly handsome face was dark in the shadowy room, his image blurred with her tears.

He did not move. He let her body adjust to the enormity of him filling her. His voice was low. "If I'd known…"

"That's why I didn't tell you."

His hands tightened on her shoulders. "I never wanted to—"

"It's done. I'm not going to let myself regret it." Blinking fast, she whispered, "Kiss me."

As he stared down at her, his expression changed. Slowly, he lowered his head. With a feather-soft touch, he kissed her eyelids, her cheeks and, finally, her lips.

She kissed him back recklessly, teasing his tongue with her own. She felt different. Nothing could take her back now to the girl she'd been. Their bodies intertwined as she deepened the kiss, tightening her hold over his shoulders, offering herself completely.

She heard the low growl from the back of his throat as he responded. The weight of his muscular body was heavy over hers. She felt him stir, hard and thick, deep, so deep inside her. A delicious tension began to coil again low in her belly.

Slowly, very gently, he began to move, sliding inside her. Pleasure filled her, even deeper than before, sending her tighter, higher. Her back arched as she met his thrusts, drawing him down inside her, twisting her hips as he pushed harder inside her.

His breath became hoarse as their rhythm increased. Her hips rose to meet him as he thrust into her hard and fast, filling every inch of her. She held her breath as the world seemed to spin, a maelstrom of white moonlight and black shadow. With a loud, guttural shout, he poured himself deep inside her, and she cried out as pleasure consumed every inch of her like fire.

Somewhere, there was a phone ringing. It kept stopping, then restarting.

Ares wished it would stop. He wanted to stay asleep, right where he was. He slowly, blearily opened his eyes.

He was in bed. Ruby was asleep in his arms, her cheek pressed against his naked chest. His arms tightened around her.

A virgin. She'd been a virgin. He still couldn't believe it. Or believe the night he'd shared with her: the single best night of his life.

He'd thought possessing her once would be enough. But now he realized that, just as when Ruby had claimed she was only coming to his house for dinner, perhaps he'd been lying to himself, as well.

Glancing at the window, he saw the sky had lightened to gray with streaks of pink. It was nearly dawn. He'd slept the whole night through, holding her in his arms. He'd never done that with any woman before, a fact that had made all his previous mistresses argue and despair. He couldn't stand for anyone to be close to him as he slept.

Until now.

Ruby was different from the rest.

More different than he'd even imagined.

Careful not to wake her, he pulled away to pick up his ringing phone from the nightstand. He saw his pilot's number. He answered the phone with a gruff "Yes?"

"Your plane is ready, sir. I know you wanted to leave as soon as possible this morning, so I'm letting you know."

"Thank you," he said, and hung up.

Ruby still slumbered trustingly beside him. Naked. And he realized to his surprise that even now, he wanted more of her. Far more.

Ares kissed her softly on the forehead to wake her. Her dark lashes fluttered as she smiled up at him dreamily.

"Hello."

"Hello," he said, running his hand down her cheek to the sensitive corner of her neck. She sighed with pleasure. He kissed her lips, exploring, teasing, tasting. Still half asleep, she started to reach her arms around him.

Then her eyes opened and she abruptly pulled away. Wide-eyed, she sat up in bed, looking at the encroaching light from the window.

"What time is it?" she said in a panic.

He shrugged lazily, soaking up the vision of her beauty as the sheet slipped low over a rosy nipple. "Night. Morning. What does it matter?"

"I didn't go home last night! My mother must be worried sick—and my sister…" She sucked in her breath, looking at him with horror. "If Ivy founds out I slept with you, after the way I yelled at her…"

"She'll be fine."

"She'll hate me!"

"I was never interested in her at all, so I don't see what she'd be angry about."

"My *hypocrisy*." Ruby got out of bed, and his gaze traced hungrily over her naked body, her full, gorgeous breasts, her tiny waist, the generous curve of her backside. "And I'm supposed to teach a kids' ski class at nine. I can't be late!"

The last thing he wanted her to do was leave his bed. "So quit that job. Stay with me."

She stared at him. "Are you crazy? I'm not going to blow off my job!"

"Quit *all* your jobs." He gave her a slow, lazy grin. "Run away with me."

Pulling on her panties, she straightened in shock. "What do you mean?"

Still stretched out on the huge bed, Ares tucked his hands behind his head. "I got a call from my pilot. My plane is ready."

"Are you going somewhere?"

"Sydney."

"Australia?"

"I'll be there a few weeks." He looked at her. "Come with me."

Ruby stared at him, swallowed, tried to speak. He saw the yearning in her dark eyes.

Then her jaw tightened. Shaking her head, she said roughly, "It's a fantasy."

"Fantasies are meant to come true."

She gave a bitter laugh. "Maybe in your world."

"So come join my world."

For a moment, Ruby stared at him. Then she shook her head with a glare. "Stop. Just stop!"

"Stop what?"

"I'm not going anywhere. I told you, my mom is sick. I'm the only one bringing in income. I can't just leave."

Ares relaxed, relieved. So it was a question of money, nothing more. For a moment he'd thought she was actually rejecting him. Financial problems were easily solved.

And if part of him felt disappointed Ruby was already asking for money, he stomped on the feeling. So she wasn't *entirely* different from other women. What had he expected? Women always wanted his money. And why wouldn't they? It was the main thing he could offer, other than sex. It wasn't like he was going to give any woman his days, his heart or his name.

Rising from bed, he pulled on his boxers and went to his desk. He only had a few thousand dollars in cash—he was on vacation after all—so he reached for a checkbook. Anachronistic, but occasionally useful. "How much money do you need?"

Awkwardly hooking the back of her bra, Ruby said blankly, "Money?"

"Yes. Fifty thousand dollars? A hundred?"

Looking at him, she stumbled back a step. "A hundred thousand dollars?"

"Is that not enough?"

"Why would you give me money? What are you paying me for?"

Ares frowned, pausing with the pen still in his hand. She didn't sound as grateful as he expected. "I just want you to come with me. To Australia."

"If you want to spend time with me, you don't have to pay anything. Just stay here!"

"In Star Valley?" He snorted. "Vacation can't last forever. I have things to do."

"So do I!"

His eyebrows lifted incredulously. "Like what? Pouring drinks? Teaching children how to ski?"

Her beautiful dark eyes turned cold as her jaw set. "Ah. So what you do is important, but what I do is not?"

"You can't seriously compare your minimum-wage jobs to running a multibillion-dollar conglomerate," he said tersely. "I have shareholders and thousands of employees. While you..."

Ruby's eyes narrowed dangerously. Still dressed in just her underwear, she folded her arms. "I what?"

Did he really have to spell it out? "Your talent is wasted here."

If her eyes had looked dangerous before, they were positively shooting sparks now. "Which talent are you talking about?"

Ares didn't understand why she seemed so angry, or why the temperature in the bedroom had suddenly turned icy. "You're better than the jobs you do, Ruby. Obviously, you deserve better."

"And by *better*—you mean instead of working honest jobs for honest pay, I should be employed full-time in your bed?"

He ground his teeth, his own temper starting to rise in turn. "That's not what I meant!"

"What else would you be paying me for?"

"I'm trying to help you out. Money is meaningless to me. Nothing but a tool to get what I want."

Ruby looked at him coldly. "There's only one tool I see, and I'm looking right at him."

His shoulders tightened. "You indicated money was an issue. I'm just trying to solve your problem."

"You're trying to buy me."

"We had a great night. I want a little more. Why are you insulted?"

"It's not me you want. You just aren't ready to let go of your toy. Because you don't even know me." She lifted her chin. Her dark eyes glittered. "If you knew me at all, you'd know I would never give up my life, my friends, my home just to be some rich man's paid mistress!"

Some rich man. He felt oddly stung by her choice of words. "You are worried about your family. I can help. That's all."

"You think money could replace me to them? You think I can just run away? My mother isn't just sick. She's dying."

"You say that like it's a bad thing," he muttered, thinking of his own parents.

It was the exact worst thing he could say.

Sucking in her breath with a furious squeak, Ruby turned and left the bedroom. Jaw clenching, he dropped the pen with a thud over his open checkbook and followed her into the enormous main room, with its magnificent view of the snowy mountain, pink with the early light of dawn.

"Stop this, Ruby," he ground out. "You're being ridiculous!"

"So now I'm ridiculous, am I?" She put on her black shirt hurriedly. "My jobs are meaningless, my family is meaningless. Nothing about me matters except that I'm useful to you in bed!"

"That's not what I said!"

She yanked up her leggings so fast she almost tripped on the white rug in front of the fire. "I was scared of being a one-night stand. I was scared of falling in love with you and having my heart broken. But this is worse. Because I'm not even a person to you, am I? I'm just a toy, to be bought and paid for!"

"That's not true!"

"You offered me a check!"

"I'm starting to regret it!"

Furious tears gleamed in her eyes. "Were you planning to pay me by the hour, or per service rendered? I'm just curious!"

"I was trying to be nice," he bit out.

"Nice? You're rubbing my face in it! You're so much more important, in every way! Look at all your money! Look at your important job running a worldwide company! Why, I should be grateful—on my hands and knees—that you'd offer to buy sex from a girl like me!"

"Ruby, damn you—"

"You're just like every rich man," she choked out, wiping her eyes. "Selfish to the core!"

Ares ground his teeth. "If that's how you feel, forget it!"

"Oh, I will!" Storming into the mudroom, she tugged on her snow boots and grabbed her wet ski clothes and bag. "Don't bother calling me, ever!"

"No problem!"

And Ruby left his house, slamming the door behind her.

Outside, Ares heard her truck start up with a low metallic roar. He heard the noise of the engine fade as she drove off. He was left alone in his enormous ski lodge, amid the cool shadows of dawn. Clawing back his hair, he looked bleakly around the gorgeous great room.

What the hell had just happened?

The gaslit fire still flickered in the white-brick fireplace, leaving shadows against his white furniture and black wood floors. Through the windows, the snow-covered mountain was rosy with soft light.

Ruby had given him the most amazing night of his life, then in the cold light of dawn rejected him completely. He felt a strange sucking sensation in his chest.

She was different after all. She hadn't wanted his money. She'd judged him for his character, for himself alone. After a hot night of passion, she'd looked into his soul to see what else was there.

And she'd seen the answer: nothing.

Well, what did he care? He didn't need her. At all. Picking up his phone, Ares dialed a number.

"Have Santos bring the car," he told his bodyguard tersely. "I want to be at the airport in ten minutes."

Ruby wiped her tears as her old truck bounced down the mountain over the icy road.

Her crying had started before the door of Ares's ski lodge even slammed closed behind her. It was why she'd had to get out of there so fast. She couldn't—wouldn't—let Ares Kourakis see her cry. Ever!

But her hands were shaking so much, it had taken her three tries to start her truck. Even now, as she gripped the steering wheel, she felt grateful for the long drive to their trailer park in Sawtooth. She couldn't let her mother see her like this.

Or worse—Ivy.

Breathing a low curse, Ruby drove swiftly through Star Valley's deserted streets at dawn.

The only people awake this early were the service workers, coming to clean the hotels and cook breakfast at the cafes. Everyone else was still asleep. Ares had probably gone back to bed himself. Why would he care that he'd hurt her so badly? He'd just find some other, prettier, more sensible lover to replace her. He'd probably already forgotten her name.

While Ruby would never be able to forget him.

She wiped her cheek with her sleeve. What had she been thinking, sleeping with a wealthy playboy?

She should have known better.

She *had* known better.

But she'd actually convinced herself that she might be some kind of exception. That some fairy tales might come true. She choked out a sob, staring at the road ahead. It had felt magical when they'd been flying down the mountain in moonlight. When he'd kissed her by the bonfire. She'd been dazzled, lost.

But she'd always known how any romance between a man like Ares Kourakis and a regular girl like her would end. Or so she'd thought.

Even Ruby had never imagined it ending with him offering her a *check*.

She drove faster, hurrying down the two-lane highway. She gulped for breath between sobs.

She'd been just sexual amusement to him. He'd taken her virginity just to see what she had on offer. Once he'd had his sample, he'd decided he was willing to buy, or at least rent.

She slowed down as she passed the small airport that served the whole valley. She saw multiple private aircraft parked on the tarmac. One was bigger than the rest, with *Kourakis Enterprises* on the side.

If she'd chosen differently, she might be climbing into that airplane right now like a princess, ready to fly across the world.

She'd actually been tempted. That was the worst part. She'd almost said yes. The money could have given her mother more comfort, better care. But Ruby couldn't pretend that was the only reason.

She'd yearned to spend time with him. To live, even briefly, in his world. To spend every night in his bed, even for a short while.

And for that, she'd almost given up everything she believed in.

The acknowledgment shamed her. Giving up her work and family to become a rich man's full-time paid mistress would have been a repudiation of everything her mother had ever taught her.

Ruby was a person, not a toy. She had a life of her own. Her family needed her. Ares either hadn't understood that, or hadn't cared. And after all her mother's warnings, Ruby had still been stupid enough to give her virginity to a coldhearted, selfish billionaire.

Tears were still streaming down her cheeks as Ruby turned into her quiet neighborhood, full of well-tended mobile homes. But as she parked outside her family's trailer, she didn't see her sister's old yellow Beetle. Strange.

Unlocking the front door, Ruby peeked inside the kitchen. There was no light anywhere.

"Hello?" she called softly, not wanting to wake her mother. "Hello?" she said more loudly.

The trailer was empty. Where were they? Remembering her sister's calls with an intake of breath, she reached into her bag and turned on her phone. She saw with mounting horror that Ivy had called ten times. And there were twice as many texts.

In a panic, Ruby didn't wait to read them but dialed her sister's number. She was relieved when Ivy answered on the second ring.

"What's wrong?" she panted.

"Where have you been?" Ivy's voice was sodden with tears.

Guilt flooded Ruby. "I'm so sorry, I—"

"It doesn't matter. You're too late. I'm at the hospital." Her little sister's voice was flat. "Mom just died."

CHAPTER FIVE

FOUR AND A half months later, dark clouds drizzled rain over Paris on a hot, humid August night as Ares left his luxury hotel on the Avenue George V. An umbrella instantly appeared over his head as he hurried to his waiting Bentley.

"Have a good trip, sir," the hotel doorman said respectfully in French.

Ares nodded, distracted by the phone pressed to his ear, as his bodyguard Georgios followed, holding the umbrella. He was already thinking about the meeting that awaited him in Mumbai tomorrow, and only half listening to his executive assistant in New York as she listed the issues needing his decision.

"And we had another call from Poppy Spencer," Dorothy added. "She wants to confirm you'll be at her charity gala on Saturday."

Ares rolled his eyes. He suspected his former mistress mostly wanted to rub her recent engagement in his face. Too bad for her he honestly didn't care. "Will I be in New York?"

"Yes, Mr. Kourakis, and many of your business associates and clients are already on the guest list. You might find the gala useful. Or even, dare I say, fun. The charity is for children who—"

"Fine," he cut her off. "Get a table."

"A good table will be expensive at this late date."

"Make it happen," he said, already bored. "Is that all?"

Dorothy grew quiet. Her silence gained his attention as nothing else could. She was always scrupulous with his time; it was one of the things that had made her such a valuable asset over the past ten years. "Dorothy? Are you there?"

"I'm not sure how to say this, sir."

"Oh, God, are you quitting?"

She snickered. "You wouldn't survive." Then she hesitated. "A woman called the company's main number an hour ago. Eventually the call escalated to me. She claims… Well, I wouldn't have believed her, except that you were in Star Valley at the time."

Star Valley. Suddenly, Ares gripped his phone. "Who called?"

"A woman by the name of—" she seemed to consult her notes "—Ruby Prescott."

Don't bother calling me. Ever.

Ares stopped on the sidewalk. The bodyguard holding the umbrella nearly walked into him. "What did she say?"

"Miss Prescott wanted to speak with you directly. But since she didn't already have your personal number, I explained you were unavailable, and suggested she leave her message with me."

He stared fixedly at the brilliant city lights reflected in the dark puddles of the Parisian street. "And?"

Dorothy took a deep breath. He'd never heard her sound so unglued about anything, not even the time the company stock had dropped so precipitously after one of their ships had sunk off the coast of South Africa. "She said she was happy not to have to talk to you. Because...um..."

"Just say it."

"She says she's pregnant. With your baby."

Ares's jaw dropped.

"That's the message," Dorothy said unhappily. "Mr. Kourakis, I'm sorry to intrude in what certainly is a very personal matter..."

Georgios opened his car door. Ares barely felt

the raindrops as he fell into the back seat of his Bentley. He was gripping the phone so hard his fingers hurt.

Pregnant.

Pregnant?

"Is there anything you want me to do, sir?"

Ares stared blankly through the window at the dark, wet streets of the 8th Arrondissement. The stately cream-and-gray belle epoque buildings shone with light. Even a nearby cathedral spire was illuminated, reaching up into the dark rainy night.

Ruby.

Pregnant.

Impossible. She couldn't be. They'd used protection.

He could still remember how he'd felt when he'd kissed her. When he'd heard her soft sigh of surrender. How she'd shuddered, crying out with pleasure in his arms. How he'd done the same.

And she'd been a virgin. He'd never been anyone's first lover. Ares had lost his virginity at eighteen, a relatively late age compared to his friends, but growing up as he had, he'd idealistically wanted to wait for love. And he had, until he'd fallen for a sexy French girl the summer after boarding school. It wasn't until summer ended that his father had gleefully revealed that Melice had actually been a prostitute, bought and paid for all the time. *I did it for your own good, boy. All that weak-minded yearning over love was getting on my nerves. Now you know what all women are after—money. You're welcome.*

Ares's bodyguard closed the car door behind him with a bang, causing him to jump.

"Sir? Are you there?"

Turning his attention back to his assistant on the phone, Ares said grimly, "Give me her phone number."

Two minutes later, as his driver pulled the sedan smoothly down the street, merging into Paris's evening traffic, Ares listened to the phone ring and ring. Why didn't Ruby answer?

When he'd left Star Valley, he'd thought he could forget her.

Instead, he'd endured four and a half months of painful celibacy, since his traitorous body didn't want any other woman. He couldn't forget the soft curves of Ruby's body, her sweet mouth like sin. She hadn't wanted his money. She'd been insulted by his offer. She'd told him never to call her again.

And now...

She was pregnant. With his baby.

He sat up straight as the phone was finally answered.

"Hello?"

A rush went through him at the sound of Ruby's low voice. He forced his own to remain cold. "Is it true?"

She didn't ask who he was or what he was talking about. "Yes."

"And you're sure the baby's mine?"

"You're the only man I've ever been with," she answered flatly, "so I'm pretty sure."

He waited, but she didn't continue. He frowned. If she was pregnant, why wasn't she making demands? He craved the chance to throw her earlier prideful rejection of his money back in her face. How he would have relished that!

But she said nothing.

"What do you want from me, Ruby? Money?" he said finally. "Because if you're thinking I'll marry you—"

"I don't want a damn thing. I just thought you should know."

And the line went dead in his hands.

Ares stared down incredulously at his phone. *She'd hung up on him.*

He blinked in shock.

If it had been any other woman, he would have been suspicious of any pregnancy claim, and certainly demanded a paternity test. But she'd rejected Ares and his money too thoroughly for him not to believe her. She obviously hated the fact that she was pregnant with his child.

As the driver drove the Bentley through Paris, heading toward the airport, Ares stared out the window at the smudged lights in the rain.

Ruby, pregnant with his baby.

His baby.

Ares took a deep breath. He knew he would be no good as a husband or father. Not after the way he'd been raised. His parents were the only example he'd had of family life. He had no desire to perpetuate that kind of misery by dragging any woman and child permanently into his life, in the zero-sum war of marriage.

No. He knew his limitations. Ruby would swiftly realize, if she hadn't already, that she was better off raising the baby alone.

But what Ares could offer was money. In fact, he would insist on it. Neither Ruby nor his child would ever be in want of anything for the rest of their lives. He would give her the ski lodge, which he'd never gotten around to selling, new cars and a large fortune. A trust fund for the baby. Ruby would never need to work again.

She would try to reject his help, as she had before. But this time he would not let her.

He was determined to provide for them. Ruby was probably working the same ridiculous jobs around the clock, even pregnant. That could be why her voice sounded so flat and tired.

Perhaps he should bring her to New York, where he could make sure she rested and took care of herself throughout the pregnancy. Her pride might try to fight him. But he would insist.

Yes. He liked the idea of bringing her back to New York. His own private kingdom.

His eyes narrowed. And he could end his obsession with Ruby Prescott once and for all.

He'd tried to forget her. Now he knew there would be no forgetting. Not until he was finally satisfied. Then, and only then, would he be free of her.

Ares would bring her to New York for the duration of her pregnancy, and while providing for her and the baby, he could tempt Ruby back to his bed. He would be finally rid of his unspeakable, inconvenient desire.

Narrowing his eyes, he dialed his executive assistant's number.

"Change my schedule," he said. "I won't be going to Mumbai tonight."

"There," Ruby snapped. "I told him about the baby. I hope you're happy."

"Happy?" Ivy stared starkly at her in their kitchen. Since the night before, when Ruby had told her she was pregnant with Ares Kourakis's baby, her sister hadn't stopped crying. "Why on earth would I be happy?"

"Because I called him like you wanted. You won!"

Slamming down a tin of freshly home-baked blueberry muffins, her little sister muttered angrily beneath her breath. All morning, Ivy had been furiously baking up a storm in the trailer's tiny kitchen, taking the cookies and cupcakes to neighbors while not letting Ruby have any and constantly yelling at her to tell Ares about the baby.

Exhausted by Ivy's harassment, Ruby had finally done it. It had given her no pleasure. Since Ares had never given her his private number, she'd been forced to call Kourakis Enterprises's main corporate office in New York. It had been humiliating to beg one stranger after another to take a message for the top boss. Finally, she'd reached his executive secretary. By then, Ruby had been so embarrassed and furious she'd just blurted out her news.

Within ten minutes, Ares himself had called her. Ivy apparently was not pleased with how Ruby had handled that brief discussion.

"I didn't win anything, and neither did you," Ivy bit out. "Telling him you didn't want a damn thing? What were you thinking?"

"I did the right thing, like you said," she told Ivy coldly. "I told him. That's the end of it. He won't care."

"But he'll pay!"

"I don't want his money." Ruby's cheeks still burned, remembering how after he'd seduced her, he'd assumed he could buy her. There was no way she'd ask him for money now and prove him right!

"You are so stupid!" Ivy covered her face with her hands. "What was the point in calling him if you were only going to brush him off?"

"To get you off my back!"

Setting her jaw, Ivy paced in front of the old fridge. "You're an idiot!"

"Why?" Ruby demanded petulantly. "Because

I'm not trying to get money from him? Because unlike some people, I have a sense of pride?"

"Pride?" Her little sister stopped, staring at her with furious blue eyes. "You'd condemn your baby into growing up like we did? With no money? How will you pay for day care?"

A nervous feeling roiled through Ruby's belly. "I'll figure it out."

"How? You have no savings. You're juggling three part-time jobs with no medical benefits. What will you do if you get sick, Ruby? What if the baby does?"

The fear in Ruby's belly increased from butterflies to rolling boulders. "I'll deal with it."

Ivy looked near tears. "Your child will be mocked at school just like we were, eating free lunch, wearing cast-off clothes—"

"I liked those castoffs," Ruby retorted. "They showed me how amazing vintage clothes can be."

Her sister glared at her. "Did you like accepting charity, as well? Did you like seeing Mom sob at night when she thought we weren't looking, when she couldn't pay our bills?"

Ruby fell silent.

"Mom worked herself to the bone, and it still wasn't enough. How do you think she liked the times she had to beg for charity and government assistance?" Ivy gave a bitter laugh. "Where will your pride be then?"

Ruby's chin sank. A wave of nausea washed over her.

Over the last months, she'd tried her best to cope. Tried to be strong. But the last of their paltry savings had been wiped out by their mother's medical expenses. For their mother's funeral, friends and neighbors had brought flowers and provided food. But even that simple service had cost money, and Ruby had no idea how she'd repay that debt.

If all that hadn't been enough, a month after their mother's death, Ruby had realized she was pregnant.

The one time she'd allowed herself to experience reckless pleasure, she'd been punished for it in every way possible. Her mother had died in the hospital without Ruby being able to say goodbye. She was still heartbroken, and for all her bravado, she was scared to death.

She'd never thought she'd repeat her mother's mistakes. But in spite of all her big dreams, here she was, shaping out to be just the same—a single mother, struggling to get by on low-wage jobs, living in a rented trailer, one unpaid bill away from disaster. And already in debt.

"When I think of how much I used to look up to you," Ivy said now, staring at her in the messy kitchen. "I thought you were so smart and strong. And now just look at you!"

"I can't ask Ares for help! I can't!"

"Are you crazy? You have to! Mom never had a choice. You do. But you won't even ask. For all you know, Ares might give you millions of dollars. He might even *marry* you."

Ruby's mouth went dry. Marriage? "Now you're the one who's crazy!"

"At the very least, he'd pay child support. And probably lots more." Ivy shook her head angrily. "You could be rich and comfortable. But no! You not only stole my dream, you're messing it all up! You're ruining your life—and your baby's!"

Was she? Suddenly shaking, Ruby stared at her sister. "But if I accepted money from him, he would own me. He might…" But she couldn't say what she feared most: that he would treat her as his toy, seduce her, make her love him. Break her heart.

"So let me get this straight," Ivy said coldly. "You won't be a gold digger, oh, no. You won't ask for marriage, you won't ask for money. You won't even ask for child support!"

"It's my life, Ivy!"

"Your baby is the one who's going to suffer for it!" Grabbing their mother's old suitcase from the closet, she started tossing stuff into it. "Well, I won't stay and watch."

"What are you doing?"

"What I should have done a long time ago," Ivy said. "Heading out on my own."

"You're leaving?"

Her sister shot her a scornful glance. "Why should I stay? Because you're such a good role model? Thanks so much for keeping me from my evil plan of getting pregnant and rich, Ruby," she said sarcastically. "Your plan was so much better—ending up pregnant and poor!"

"I didn't plan for any of this to happen!"

"No. You just blundered your way into it." Ivy pulled her suitcase down the shag carpeting of the hallway to her bedroom. "And I'm not going to let you drag me down with you!"

She was just upset, Ruby told herself desperately. Ivy had been furious when she'd told her about the pregnancy. She'd had no choice; her belly was starting to show. But surely, once Ivy had a chance to think, she would calm down.

Nervously, Ruby started tidying her sister's dirty dishes in the kitchen. But by the time she'd washed all the dishes, put away the flour and sugar and wiped down the counters, her sister had packed up her old yellow Beetle with all the clothes, shoes and boxes that would fit.

Coming back into the kitchen, Ivy put the freshly baked muffins into a brown paper bag. Facing her sister, she twisted her car keys in her hands. "So I guess this is goodbye."

A lump rose in Ruby's throat. "Please don't go," she whispered. "I can't lose you, too."

Ivy looked back at her. "Don't force your baby to live in poverty, Ruby. That's the wrong kind of pride."

And with that, her nineteen-year-old sister departed, leaving Ruby standing alone and uncertain in the trailer's worn kitchen.

She heard the Beetle drive away. The trailer suddenly felt quiet. She could hear Mr. Rafferty's dog barking down the street.

Nausea roiled her. She leaned her hands against the peeling countertop for support. She'd called in sick today from all three jobs. She'd barely slept last night, and had woken to more morning sickness. It had already forced her to miss multiple days of work over the last few months. None of her jobs had sick leave, which meant her paycheck was smaller. She was falling deeper and deeper into debt. And her baby hadn't even been born yet.

What will you do if you get sick, Ruby?

Closing her eyes, she leaned her forehead against the cool white fridge, waiting for the waves of nausea to pass. But it just got worse. She ran to the bathroom, making it just in time. Brushing her teeth afterward, she looked at herself in the mirror. The doctor had said the nausea should be getting better by now, but it hadn't yet. She took a long shower, trying to wash away her anxiety and fear.

I'll figure it out, Ruby told herself as she got into clean pajamas. I just need a plan. Grabbing a box of saltines, a notebook and a pen, she went to the couch. Breathing deeply, she drank some water and ate crackers to settle her stomach. She stared hard at the blank page. She just had to come up with a plan…a plan…

Hours later, she woke up, sleepy and disoriented. The living room was totally dark. Someone was banging the front door in the middle of the night. She exhaled. Ivy had come back!

Pushing her blanket aside, Ruby rushed to the front door, nearly tripping over her own feet. She flung it open.

But it wasn't Ivy.

Ares Kourakis stood at her doorway, all hard edges and hulking shoulders. Parked behind him was the gleaming outline of a black sports car, and behind that, a black SUV with a large man standing beside it, arms folded.

"Hello, Ruby."

Staring up at Ares, she stammered, "What are you doing here?"

His sensual lips curved. "You called me."

"I never expected—"

"What?" he bit out. "You never expected I would want to provide for my child?"

Glowering, he strode past her into the trailer. Shocked, she fell back, facing him in her shadowy kitchen.

Ares. Here. Now. Ruby couldn't look away from him, so tall and broad, handsome and sleek in his well-cut dark clothes. His presence overwhelmed her. "I th-thought you were in Paris."

"You think I could have been anywhere in the world and not have tracked you down after you hung up on me?"

"I…"

He was close enough to touch, looking down at her in the enclosed space of the tiny kitchen. His dark hair was slightly longer than she remembered, adding a hint of wave, of wild unpredictability, to his civilized appearance. As if beneath the tailored clothes, he was a barbarian who might do anything.

Which was exactly what he was. A barbarian who used his money like a weapon to get what he wanted.

He moved closer. "Have you seen a doctor?"

"Of course I have!" she said, then added softly, "Once."

"Just once?"

"It's expensive," she said defensively. "But I got the vitamins and everything…"

"Have you been taking them?"

She bit her lip. "I've had morning sickness. Sometimes it's hard to keep vitamins down. There've been a few times I've had to call in sick from work…"

"That stops now."

"Calling in sick?"

"Working. I've already phoned your employers and informed them that you will no longer be working for any of them."

Ruby drew back with a savage intake of breath before she exploded, "You did *what*?"

He glowered down at her. "Did you really think I would just disappear?"

"So you made it impossible for me to provide for my baby?"

"From now on, that's my job."

"You bastard!" she raged. Angry tears lifted to her eyes. "How could you?"

"Easily. Now you are pregnant with my child…" His gaze traced over her swollen breasts and the hint of her belly beneath her pajamas. Reaching out, he cupped her cheek as he growled, "You no longer have the right to deny me."

Even panting with rage, Ruby felt his fingertips against her skin and shivered with humiliating desire. She'd tried so hard to hate him since their night together. She nearly succeeded during daylight hours, when she was busy with work and could remind herself of good reasons to despise him. The coldhearted way he'd said that her mother's death would be a *good* thing. How he'd actually tried to pay Ruby to abandon her family.

But at night, dreams of Ares still haunted her,

hot memories of his hard body against hers, of his voice, husky in the darkness, telling her he wanted her. And now his baby was growing deep inside her.

"You don't understand." Ruby's voice cracked. "I'm barely getting by. My mother's medical bills wiped us out. I had to borrow money for her funeral—"

"Funeral?"

Ruby closed her eyes. "She died the night you and I were together. I only found out after...after it was too late."

"I'm sorry," he said in a low voice. His hand moved from her cheek to her shoulder. "I know how much you loved her."

For a moment, Ruby accepted his comfort. Then she pulled away. She couldn't let him know. Couldn't let him see how he affected her even now. As their eyes locked in the shadowy kitchen, her heart was pounding. Her body, already flooded with adrenaline and pregnancy hormones, had revved from zero to one hundred faster than his sports car outside.

"It was even harder on Ivy," she whispered. "She is so young..."

Then she remembered, and her voice choked off.

"Has she been taking good care of you?"

A lump rose in her throat. "Ivy just moved out. She was furious to discover I was pregnant. And even more angry that I didn't ask you for money when I called." She gave a bitter laugh. "She said I'd not only stolen her dream, I'd messed it all up."

Ares looked down at her. "Did you?"

"Did I what?"

"Did you steal her dream?"

"What do you mean?"

"Did you get pregnant on purpose?"

She sucked in her breath. "Of course not!"

Ares's dark eyes traced her face, then he shook his head. "If it were any other woman, I might wonder. But not you." His lips lifted cynically on the edges. "You obviously are not thrilled about it."

Her hands gently covered the soft swell of her belly beneath her pajamas. "I already love this baby. But…"

"But you hate that I'm the father."

She looked down. "I don't…hate you…exactly."

"You don't?" he said softly.

Ruby lifted her chin. "But I hate your selfishness. Your cold arrogance. I hate that you offered to pay me to abandon my dying mother. So I could travel the world like your sex toy."

His jaw tightened. "That's not how I saw it."

"If you wanted to see me again after our night together, you should have asked me on a date. Not offered to write me a check, then when I was upset, calmly explained that my mother's death would actually be a good thing."

"I was trying to comfort you."

"Comfort!" she gasped.

"Yes," he said shortly. "My own life was far better after my parents died."

Ruby's jaw dropped. She saw from his expression that he was serious. "That's a horrible thing to say."

His dark eyes were cold. "It's a horrible thing to be true." He came closer in the darkened kitchen, his powerful body encroaching on her personal space. "You will pack your bags."

"Pack? For where?"

"New York."

"I'm not going to New York!"

"Since I cannot trust you to take care of yourself, or even to take my money, you will be under my care for the rest of your pregnancy." He was so close. Her senses were screaming, "Danger" even as her nerve endings hummed with longing and need. He continued flatly, "You have no other choice."

Ruby stiffened. "You made sure of that, didn't you? When you quit all my jobs behind my back!"

"For your own good."

"*My* good?"

"Why are you fighting me, Ruby?" he said impatiently. "Do you really think it would be better to struggle through your pregnancy in exhaustion and unpaid bills? You think that's how I want my child to be raised?"

"I've seen what happens when a rich man gets bored with his promises," she whispered. She shook her head. "In a few days or weeks you'll change your mind and toss me back on the street. I'll have no money, no job! I'll be even worse off than I am now!"

His dark eyes glittered. "Do not insult me. I will always provide for you both."

"I'm not going to New York. You and I barely know each other. And what we do know, we don't like!"

His cruel, sensual lips curved. Drawing close, until their bodies were an inch apart in the darkened kitchen, he looked down at her. He said softly, "There are a few things we liked well enough."

A shiver went through her, creating little cascades of need across her body. As his dark eyes held hers, all she could remember was the explosive night that had created a child against all odds. The breathless hush of heat, of naked passion in the flickering light of the fire on that cold winter's night.

No! She couldn't let herself remember. She couldn't let herself feel. She couldn't let herself want him.

"At the end of your pregnancy, you may return to Star Valley, if you choose." He looked slowly over her old, peeling kitchen. "You will have the deed to my ski lodge, along with a generous income to maintain it. And anything else you desire."

Ares was trying to give her his thirty-million-dollar house? She felt suddenly faint. "I…I'm not taking it."

"Why?"

"Because…" She put her hand to her forehead, feeling dizzy. "Nothing comes for free."

"Let's be honest, Ruby. As you said, I am selfish. Cold. There are some things I cannot offer you," he said in a low voice. "Love. Marriage." His lips curved harshly. "And we both know I won't be much of a father."

Ruby stared at him. His voice sounded so haunted. So…empty. "How do you know? Do you have other children?"

He shook his head. "I've always been careful."

"You and I were careful," she pointed out.

"Ah." He gave a small smile. "But if any other woman had gotten pregnant, she would have immediately tried to cash in."

"I'm not trying to cash in," she said, insulted.

"I wish you were. Money is easy to give. At least it would be, with any other woman but you." His jaw set. "I will take no more of your insults, asking if I intend to abandon you and my child to poverty," he said grimly. "Now go get dressed."

The floor seemed to tremble beneath her. "I won't go."

"Your mother is dead, Ruby. Your sister is gone. Why are you desperate to stay?" He paused. "Or are you just afraid to be alone with me?"

Terrified. But she lifted her chin. "Why would I be?"

"I can call in my bodyguard and have him physically carry you to the car, if necessary. But one way or the other, you will obey me." He turned away. "On second thought, don't bother packing. I will have new clothes waiting for you in New York."

Ruby glanced down at her bright pink pajamas, which were so soft and always comforted her. "What's wrong with the clothes I already have?"

"You have two minutes," he said flatly.

"Until what?"

"Until I send in Georgios to carry you out like a sack of potatoes. If any of your neighbors are awake, I'm sure they'd find it very entertaining." He turned to the door. "I'll be outside."

Exactly two minutes later, Ruby came out in clean clothes, an outfit she loved: stretchy, bright purple cutoffs and a vintage 1980s T-shirt with a big rainbow across the front, stretching over her baby bump. Locking the trailer door behind her, she pulled her freshly brushed hair back into a ponytail with a bright yellow bow and lifted her canvas bag to her shoulder.

Ares was already in the Lamborghini, with his bodyguard in the big SUV behind.

"I hate you," she grumbled as she climbed in beside him.

"It's for your own good."

"Say that one more time, and I might slap you."

Ares's gaze traced over her lazily, then revved the engine. "Looking forward to it."

He pushed down on the gas. The two vehicles drove through the trailer park and the village of Sawtooth, then out onto the two-lane state highway.

Outside, the summer night was cool. Rolling down her window, Ruby saw the dark shadow of the mountains beneath a cloudless sky of spread-out stars and bright moon. She took a deep breath of the cool air. She could smell pine trees, the river, the cottonwoods. At the thought of leaving the valley, she felt a pang of homesickness, even fear. New York. With Ares Kourakis.

As they arrived at the small regional airport, Ruby saw the enormous Kourakis Enterprises jet like a leviathan on the tarmac. As they drew closer, the jet only seemed to get bigger. Her lips parted in awe as he drove the sleek black car to a stop beside it.

Several people were waiting to meet them at the bottom of the jet's steps. A gray-haired man stepped forward with a smile.

"This is Mr. Martin, my lodge's caretaker," Ares said. "He and his wife will take care of everything you're leaving behind, your trailer, your truck. Any bills that haven't been paid. Give him your keys."

Ruby fumbled in her canvas bag for the beaded key ring Ivy had made for her as a birthday gift years earlier. The man took it with a smile. "Now, don't you worry about a thing, Miss Prescott. We'll keep an eye on everything."

As the caretaker departed, Ruby realized she was shaking in the cool night at the thought of how much she was giving away. How much she'd lost already. She breathed to Ares, "Maybe this is a mistake."

"Too late."

"I changed my mind—"

"No." Ares came closer to her. Having him so close made her suddenly nervous on every level. His dark eyes glinted dangerously in the moonlight. "Get on the plane."

"I'm scared," she whispered, trying to hide the rapid beat of her heart.

"I know." Reaching down, he cupped her cheek, stroking her tender bottom lip with the rough skin of his thumb. Leaning forward, he whispered, "We both know there is unfinished business between us."

His touch burned her cheek, causing spirals of

electricity to spin down her body, to her breasts, to her core. For a moment, she couldn't breathe. From a distance, she heard night birds singing in the darkness.

Then he turned away.

Her eyes followed him as he walked up the steps to the jet. She couldn't look away from his broad shoulders, his hard, muscular shape in those form-fitting trousers.

Ruby put her hand on her forehead. Oh, dear heaven, what had she done? Why had she ever given herself to a man like this? Why had she ever slept with him?

He was right. She did need his help, as much as she hated to admit it. But New York was not her idea. He'd bullied and blackmailed her into it.

She would go, for their baby's sake. But she wouldn't sleep with Ares again. She *wouldn't*. Sex wasn't part of the deal. She'd make that clear.

Squaring her shoulders, Ruby lifted her chin and followed him up the steps, proud as a queen. But as she stepped inside his private jet, she froze, her eyes wide.

This was nothing like her previous experience flying in the middle seat in economy class.

Ares's private jet was all elegance and open

space. As with his ski lodge, the decor was black-and-white. Black cabinets. White leather sofas.

A smiling, uniformed flight attendant greeted her warmly. "Welcome aboard, Miss Prescott. May I take your bag?"

"No," Ruby said, clinging to her colorful canvas bag. Ares had told her not to pack anything, so she'd brought only her wallet, with its five dollars and twenty-two cents, her phone and charger, a box of old family photos and a bright fuchsia Star Valley sweatshirt in case she got cold on the flight. She had so few possessions now. She wasn't going to part with any of them.

"Of course." Still smiling, the blonde woman held out an iced drink in a crystal goblet on a silver tray. "Would you care for some sparkling water, Miss Prescott? Or something else?"

"This is lovely, thank you," Ruby said, taking the glass off the tray. She glanced behind her at the burly dark-haired man who'd just boarded the plane.

"This is Georgios, my bodyguard," said Ares, who had already sat down at a nearby table and opened his computer.

"Hello, miss," the man said to Ruby with a smile that made him look much less fearsome.

"Hello." She glanced at Ares. "Why do you need a bodyguard?"

He shrugged. "It makes life easier."

"I'm an all-round assistant, really," Georgios said. "Please let me know, miss, if you ever need anything. Excuse me. I need to phone my wife." And with a slight bow, he disappeared to a separate compartment at the front of the plane.

"And I'm here to make you as comfortable as possible," the flight attendant chirped. "Anything you need, Miss Prescott, anything at all, just tell me and I'll make it happen!"

Ruby said with a snort, "In that case, I'll have some lobster thermidor and fresh blueberries, please."

The flight attendant beamed, as if it was the single happiest moment of her life. "Of course! Shall I start preparing them now?"

Ruby's grin dropped, along with her jaw. She had no idea what lobster thermidor even tasted like. It was just the most outlandish dish that she'd ever heard of. "I was joking!"

"Never joke with staff," Ares said sharply. He nodded at the flight attendant. "Thank you, Michelle. You may go."

"Yes, sir."

With a smile, the flight attendant disappeared to the front of the jet.

Frowning, Ruby stared after her. "Is she for real?"

Leaning back in his white leather seat, Ares looked at her seriously. "I don't think you realize how much your life has just changed."

She felt pierced by his dark eyes, as if he could see her soul. As if he could see straight to the corner of her heart that she did not want him to see. The side that had spent months dreaming of him. Turning away, she took a long drink of the sparkling water, avoiding his eyes. "Why? Because you're so rich?"

"Because you're pregnant with my baby." He frowned. "You will live as I live. In a life of luxury and comfort. No more low-wage jobs. No more slaving away for bosses. From now on, you're at no one's beck and call." He paused. "Except mine."

She turned to him, trying to hide the tumult of emotions inside her. "I'm pregnant with your baby, yes. And yes, I'll admit there's still a certain...attraction between us. But let's get one thing straight, Ares. I don't belong to you. I'll let you provide for us, since you've left me no option. But it doesn't mean you're buying me in the bargain. I'm not going to sleep with you."

She was proud of how steady her voice sounded.

His eyebrows lifted as he said mildly, "I've heard that before."

Ruby's cheeks went hot as she remembered how she'd told him at the Atlas Club that she was *impossible* to get—right before falling into his bed. Folding her arms, Ruby looked down at her cheap, colorful canvas sneakers against the expensively sleek gray floor of the jet. "I've learned the cost of being reckless."

Ares rose to his feet. Crossing the jet's wide cabin, he pulled her into his powerful arms.

"Your whole life, Ruby," he said huskily, "you've taken care of everyone else. Your mother. Your sister. But that is over. You don't have to fight anymore. I will take care of you now. And the baby. You're both safe now. You can rest."

Cradled in his powerful arms, Ruby felt sudden tears in her eyes. She'd longed to hear those words her whole life. Even her mother, who'd loved her so much, hadn't been able to say that, as she'd needed Ruby's help taking care of Ivy just for their family to survive.

I will take care of you now.

The desire to just let go, to let someone else be in charge, was almost irresistible.

Ares wanted to provide for her and the baby. He'd come all this way to claim her. That already made him different from her father, and Ivy's. It already made him different from Braden.

Ares had made it clear he wished to provide for their child. In fact, he was insisting on it.

But Ruby couldn't fool herself that he was the type of man who would ever be faithful to one woman. He'd said it himself—he didn't do love or marriage. He didn't even have the desire to try to be a real father. Money was all he could give.

Fine. She'd let him do that. But she wouldn't think, not even for a second, that he could ever offer more.

Once their baby was born, or perhaps sooner, he'd grow tired of her and she'd be packed back to Star Valley. He'd said it clearly. He could offer only money.

While she—she had nothing to offer but her heart.

But as Ares's hands slowly stroked up her arms, Ruby still couldn't push him away.

I will take care of you now.

Since Bonnie's death, Ruby had struggled for months in silence, with no one to turn to. She'd been pregnant alone, and paid the bills alone.

Today, even her sister had turned on her. Ruby felt like she'd had her fists up so long, she could hardly remember what it felt like to put them down.

"It's all right," Ares murmured softly, and Ruby realized she was crying, and not the pretty kind of crying, either. She was sobbing, gulping for breath. He comforted her, kissing her forehead, her cheeks. "It's all right. You're safe now. I'll take care of you and the baby. I'll take care of everything."

Ares felt so strong. So powerful. Ruby closed her eyes, pressing her cheek against his chest. She felt the soothing stroke of his hands against her back. Her shivering ceased, and her sobs quieted. The only sound was the low hum of the jet's engine.

Then she looked up. Their eyes met. And she felt something entirely different from comfort: a hot spark of need. As his gaze fell to her lips, electricity suddenly crackled between them.

"Mr. Kourakis, we are ready for takeoff." The voice of the pilot came over the intercom. "You might wish to be seated."

Her cheeks aflame, Ruby wrenched away, fleeing to the chair on the farthest edge of the cabin. Clenching both the armrests, she stared hard out the window, praying Ares wouldn't come over.

He didn't. He went back to his own chair without a word. The jet's engine roared as they moved down the runway. Ruby looked out the porthole window at they went past the small airport terminal. Past scattered buildings, going by faster and faster. Past the slender sliver of road. Past soft green cottonwoods and pine trees. Past her grief over her mother. Her guilt over her sister. Past the unpaid bills, the debt, the exhaustion and fear. Ruby was leaving it all behind.

The jet went faster and faster, until, with a rush of speed and bump of the wheels, they lifted past the jagged mountains and soared up into the blue Idaho sky.

CHAPTER SIX

"I CAN'T BELIEVE I'm here," Ruby breathed.

As their Rolls-Royce crossed the George Washington Bridge, traveling from the small airport in New Jersey to the island of Manhattan, Ruby's eyes were wide as she craned her head, looking south toward the New York City skyline. Ares enjoyed seeing her pleasure.

He intended to give her a great deal more of it.

In the back seat of the sedan, their bodies were close, but not touching. Every part of him felt aware of her. He remembered how she'd trembled in his arms before his jet had taken off from Star Valley. How she'd looked up at him, her beautiful dark eyes still shining with tears, her full pink lips parting with unconscious invitation.

If not for the interruption of the pilot, he might have kissed her right then and there, then carried her back to the bedroom to ravish her at thirty thousand feet. But she'd fled to a far chair to stare furiously out the window. As soon as the jet leveled off, Ruby had disappeared to the cabin's back bedroom alone, claiming exhaustion.

But he'd known what it really was. Fear.

She was right to be afraid. His conquest of her had only just begun.

"Oh! It's so beautiful," Ruby said as they traveled southward through the city.

"Isn't it?" He allowed himself a smile. Even New York City seemed to be conspiring in his seduction. The early-morning sun sparkled gold over the Hudson River, trailing pink across the clouds and shimmering against the buildings. He couldn't have planned it better.

She turned to him, her eyes wide. "How long have you lived here?"

"I first visited this city at twelve, after my parents sent me to boarding school in Connecticut. I often visited the city on school trips. I had the same reaction you're having now. I was dazzled by New York's energy, by its raw ambition. I moved here permanently at twenty-two, after my father died. I inherited the company and moved the headquarters from Athens."

"You moved your whole company?"

"I wanted a change." At her questioning look,

he said smoothly, "To announce the beginning of a new global era for Kourakis Enterprises."

"But Athens is also a very big city—"

"I needed a change," he said harshly.

He saw a shutter go down over her eyes.

Without a word of apology, Ares turned away. He couldn't explain. After his disastrous affair at eighteen with the French girl, who'd disappeared the instant his father paid her off, he'd sworn off love. That had lasted until, right before his final year at Princeton, he'd fallen for a Greek girl with neither Melice's sultry charms nor his mother's cold glamour. The daughter of a butcher in Pláka, Diantha was young, wholesome and virginal. He respected her decision to wait until marriage before she surrendered her virginity, because he'd once wanted the same. He planned to propose as soon as he graduated from college, even if his parents disinherited him for it.

Then his father had died suddenly, causing Ares to come back to Athens early. Going to her family's stone house in the tightly winding streets on the eastern slope of the Acropolis, he'd surprised Diantha in the arms of the butcher's young apprentice.

"Well, what did you expect, that I'd save my virginity forever?" she'd demanded. "I haven't seen you for months. I need love now. I couldn't wait forever for you to propose, no matter how rich you might be!"

It was then Ares had realized that his father had been right about love. In fact, the lessons of his parents and the rules of New York City were exactly the same.

Never leave yourself vulnerable. Never trust anyone. Lock all your feelings deep down inside, or better yet, don't have any.

Ares glanced at Ruby beside him in the back seat of the Rolls-Royce. She was craning her head right and left as they turned off the Hudson Parkway onto West 79th Street. She gaped like a child at the tall residential buildings of the Upper West Side.

She finally pointed at a large stone building, surrounded by greenery. "What's that?"

"The American Museum of Natural History."

She yelped. "The place with the big dinosaur skeletons? Like in *Night at the Museum*?"

"Yes."

"I loved that movie as a teenager. And look at all those trees!" Leaning forward with an impish grin, she confided, "I didn't think there would be trees in New York."

Her innocent pleasure warmed him. "Just wait."

From the moment he'd first seen her in the Atlas Club, he'd known Ruby was different. Honest, sometimes a little too honest. But kind. Innocent.

But he'd thought that about a woman before. Ares's smile faded.

He would have to be careful.

Because Ruby somehow made him different, too. Made him lose his edge. Made him lower his defenses. Made him stupidly want to trust her.

But every time he trusted anyone, he'd been betrayed.

He would never let himself care for Ruby, he told himself fiercely. It was impossible. He would force her and their child to take his money, yes. And he planned to seduce her and enjoy her in bed. But that was it. Everything else had been burned out of him long ago.

A yellow taxi cut them off, forcing Horace, his grizzled, battle-hardened driver, to dart into another lane. Leaning forward, Ruby gasped, "How can you drive in this traffic? You are amazing!"

Even Horace couldn't help but preen beneath Ruby's glowing praise. Until he caught his boss's eye in the rearview mirror, and coughed. "I'm used to it, Miss Prescott. You should see Mr. Kourakis drive. He could compete at the Grand Prix."

"Really?" She turned to Ares, her lovely face skeptical. "Why don't you drive yourself, then?"

"I have too much work to do."

"Oh, right. Your *superimportant* work leading your *superimportant* company."

He sensed sarcasm.

"My company does employ a hundred thousand people," he said mildly.

She opened her mouth. Then she closed it with a snap.

"Oh" was all she said.

"Oh?"

She mumbled something.

"What was that?"

"I *said*, I guess your company is a little important."

"Thanks. Kourakis Enterprises just had its most profitable year."

"I'm glad. For your employees' sake, I mean."

"You should be glad for our child's. Because who do you think will inherit after I die?"

He heard her soft gasp. "But—"

"You thought New York City had no trees?" Deliberately changing the subject, he rolled down the window as they turned onto the road that twisted into Central Park. "Look at this."

With an intake of breath, Ruby looked out as they drove down a hill, their road boxed with rough stone walls. Huge green trees peered down at them on both sides like arboreal skyscrapers, a dramatic slash against the brilliant blue sky. They traveled beneath multiple stone bridges, all of them covered with trees. Emerald leaves trailed over the medieval-looking stone walls, shimmering with dappled light.

"It's like a forest," she breathed.

"You can't see it from here, but Central Park also has lakes, and a huge open lawn with twenty-six baseball fields..."

"Twenty-six?" she gasped.

"And an open-air amphitheater for Shakespeare under the stars." He flashed her a grin. "There's a castle, too."

She looked at him accusingly. "You're joking."

"It's true."

"There's no way this park has its own *castle*."

"Star Valley isn't the only beautiful place in the world," he said smugly.

On the other side of Central Park, they drove into the Upper East Side. His driver finally pulled the sedan to a stop in front of a six-story, hundred-year-old mansion. Georgios leaped out to open her door.

"Thank you," she said, smiling as the man took her hand.

Ares ground his teeth. He trusted his bodyguard implicitly, but he didn't like watching another man touch Ruby, even to help her out of the car. Ares couldn't remember the last time he'd felt so possessive.

Never, he thought.

"Thank you, Georgios," Ares told him coldly. Reaching out, he folded her hand over his arm. "I'll take it from here."

Ruby's neck tilted back as she looked up at the elegant limestone mansion. "This is all yours?"

"Yes."

"The whole thing?" Her voice sounded strangled.

"I only want the best." He led her up the steps to where his housekeeper was waiting.

"Welcome home, sir." Tall and thin to the point of boniness, Mrs. Ford, with her perfectly coiffed white hair, could have been any age from fifty to eighty. With impeccable references, she'd made it clear in their first interview that if she chose to work for him, she'd be the one doing him the favor.

He'd liked her standoffish manner, so he'd hired her. That was eight years ago.

"Good evening, Mrs. Ford. Ruby, this is my housekeeper, Margaret Ford."

"Lovely to meet you, Miss Prescott. Welcome," the housekeeper said, her tone implying the opposite.

"Nice to meet you," Ruby replied nervously.

"I trust everything is ready?"

Mrs. Ford held the door wide. "Of course, sir."

Still holding Ruby's arm, he led her inside. And she gave a choked gasp.

Tilting her head back, she stared at the enormous crystal chandelier soaring above them in the foyer. "And I thought your lodge in Star Valley was nice."

"That?" His lips curved up on the edges. "That was just a place to rough it on ski weekends."

He was only half joking. As he led her out of the foyer, she looked at the sweeping double staircase, two stories high, and gave an astonished laugh. "I'm scared. I might get lost trying to find my room. Is there a map? Can I get directions on my phone?"

"I'll show you."

Ruby snorted. "Thanks. I'm afraid I might disappear down some hallway and never find my way back again!"

"I'd never let that happen." Having her arm wrapped over his, even over his shirt, made his body hum in anticipation. He knew this house would impress her. It impressed every woman. Usually tours ended in his bed, with no further seduction required. He suspected Ruby would require more effort. But he knew this enormous mansion would be a good start.

Giving her a sensual smile, he led her past the staircase and deliberately took her to the ballroom, the biggest and most magnificent room in the mansion. "This house was built by a steel tycoon at the turn of the last century." He pointed at the chandeliers twenty feet above. "Those were handmade in Vienna in 1902. This ballroom is the only room I didn't change. It's considered a beaux arts masterpiece."

Her forehead furrowed as she looked up, puzzled, at the elaborate fresco on the ceiling. "What on earth is it for?"

"What?"

"A ballroom." She looked at him blankly. "It must cost you a fortune to keep it cool in summer and warm in winter. You could stick three houses in here. And what do you even use it for?"

He stopped, momentarily nonplussed. Then he said, "Parties."

"Do you have a lot of parties?"

"A few."

"Birthday get-togethers?"

"Charity galas. Business functions."

"Oh." Her pink lips twisted upward. "Fun."

"It is," he lied, annoyed that she didn't seem more impressed. People were usually awed by this. But as Ruby yawned, he noticed dark circles under her eyes. "Don't worry," he said roughly. "There's more."

He led her to the huge formal dining room, with its white marble fireplace and black-and-white-checkered floor. At the center of the room, covered by an elaborate antique vase filled with fresh flowers, was a long oak table, big enough to seat eighteen.

She frowned at it. "You eat your cereal in here?"

He sighed.

"Come on," he said irritably.

Next, he led her down the hall to the huge, commercial-grade kitchen with white walls and high-end appliances. Sunlight shone through the back window, where they had their own garden, rare for the Upper East Side. He smiled. "Mrs. Ford raises fresh herbs and vegetables, along with flowers. She uses them in her cooking."

"Does she? How clever. I can't even imagine. I told you I'm not much of a cook. Pasta from a box."

"And I'm sandwiches." He grinned. "Fine pair we make."

"Pasta is harder," she said archly. "You have to boil water. So I'm a better cook than you."

Ares took a step toward her in the white, sunlit kitchen.

"I don't know," he said huskily, looking down at her. "You seemed to think my sandwich was pretty spectacular."

He heard her soft intake of breath. Her cheeks went pink as she turned away, and he knew that she, too, was remembering their night together.

She cleared her throat. "Um…so what else?"

Ares hid a smile. Taking her hand, he led her up the sweeping staircase to the second floor, which held the library, the billiards room, his home office and a solarium, fitted with an entire wall of glass overlooking the garden. But she seemed more puzzled than awed as she looked around. "Did you run out of money before you could buy furniture?"

"What do you mean?"

"The rooms are all so empty."

Ares looked around the solarium, with its white tile floor and single hard-backed white loveseat edged in chrome. The sliding glass doors led out to a back balcony with two black chairs and a black container that held ghostly white flowers.

"It's a look," he said stiffly.

Her expression was skeptical. "A look?"

"Created to my express specifications by the best designer in New York. Spartan and modern, with clean lines and plenty of space. Space is what I care about."

She rolled her eyes. "Space just means there's nothing there. How big is this place, anyway?"

"Six stories plus a basement and roof terrace. Ten bedrooms, twelve bathrooms."

Her eyes were huge. "All just for you?"

"Mrs. Ford lives on the fourth floor. Three other staff members also work here full-time, but live out."

She looked around the solarium. "It's like a hotel. A really elegant, really empty hotel."

He'd never seen any woman so unenthused by his home, which was generally considered to be a Park Avenue showplace. He said grumpily, "You haven't seen the home theater and wine cellar. The exercise room has weights and a yoga room, and there's a rooftop terrace with an arboretum and pool—"

"Please," she begged. "Just show me to my room. It was a long night. I'd like nothing more than a nap and maybe a bath."

Looking at Ruby, he paused, looking at the dark smudges beneath her beautiful brown eyes. Her cheeks were pale. "Didn't you sleep well on the plane?"

"Not very."

"As you wish," he said reluctantly. He took her to the elevator. She made no comment on it. Pressing the button for the sixth floor, he led her down the hall, and pushed open the first door to the left, revealing an enormous bedroom that was empty except for a large black four-poster bed.

"This is mine," he said.

She drew back indignantly. "You can't think—"

"I don't," he cut her off. At least, he added silently, not yet. "I just wanted you to know where I'll be. You're next door." He led her down the hall. "This is yours."

With a nervous glance, she went past him into the guest bedroom.

Of the many rooms in the house, he'd chosen this one because it was close to his, with a fine view of the city through high windows. The decor was spare, just like in the rest of the house. The center of the room held a large four-poster bed, covered with a plain white bedspread. An angular metal lamp was set on the black nightstand, which had a hidden intercom and electric plug for her phone. A hard-edged metal chandelier hung from the sculptured plaster ceiling.

She looked around her uncertainly.

"You have your own bathroom here," he said, nudging open a door with a brief smile. "Anything you might need has been provided. There's even scented bubble bath, if you're so inclined."

She looked at the dark floor.

"What's wrong?" he demanded.

Ruby looked back at him. "I just figured out what's bothering me about this place."

"My house?"

"Yeah. This whole mansion of yours. It's not just empty. It's cold. And I don't mean temperature. Other than the ballroom, there's no color. It's all black-and-white."

"Those are my favorite colors."

"They aren't colors. I have more color on my body than you do in this whole house."

Ares looked at her. It was true. Ruby was a vivid slash of color in a sea of black-and-white. She was wearing the same clothes as when she'd left Star Valley, a vintage rainbow T-shirt pulled snug over her full breasts and slight bump, and bright purple cut-off shorts. A bright yellow ribbon tied back her long dark hair. Her canvas sneakers were embroidered with flowers.

He looked down at his own well-tailored clothes. Black shirt. Black trousers. Black socks and shoes. He fit in here perfectly.

"So you hate my house," he said.

"Um. I guess I do." She gave him an apologetic smile. "Sorry."

"It's fine." Suppressing his disappointment, Ares went toward the closet door. "Maybe you'll approve of this."

Curiously, she followed him into the enormous walk-in closet, with four walls of clothing, handbags and shoes, and a center island for lingerie and accessories.

Ruby looked around in shock. "What is all this?"

"I told you I'd arrange new clothes," he said. At last, she seemed impressed by something.

"This closet is bigger than my bedroom and Ivy's put together," she said in awe.

"Maternity clothing from the best boutiques in the city." He motioned toward one wall. "You have ten different bags for every occasion. This particular one—" he touched a ladylike black bag "—is by Hermès. My executive assistant told me Princess Grace used a bag just like this to hide her pregnancy from photographers." He smiled, turning back to Ruby. "So I bought you five—"

His voice cut off. Ruby didn't look pleased, as he'd expected, at such thoughtful extravagance. She didn't touch anything, not the clothes or shoes or bags. She just stood there in her ridiculous rainbow shirt and purple shorts, her expression troubled.

"You don't like them?" he said.

"The clothes—they're just like your house." Her voice was strained. "No color. Just black-and-white."

"That's not true," he said, stung. "There's also gray. And beige!"

"Beige." She gave a visible shudder, then her shoulders tightened. "And how much did it all cost?"

"Cost?" he said blankly.

"Yes, cost. Enough to buy my trailer back home? Enough to send Ivy to college for a year? Enough to pay medical expenses for our baby's birth? Enough to put something by, in case something bad happens? Because it always does!"

Instead of being pleased, Ruby looked like she was about to burst into tears.

Ares looked around the closet he'd asked his executive assistant to arrange for her. Dorothy had spent much of last night organizing it. He thought of all the trouble and expense. He'd thought it would delight Ruby. That it would make her comfortable in the city, that it might even help him seduce her.

She'd thrown it all back in his face.

A strange emotion filled him. Something he didn't want to define. Something that he hadn't let himself feel in a long, long time.

Then he shook his head, clawing back his dark hair. Of course Ruby wouldn't let him spend money on her. Not ostentatiously and blatantly like this. For a man who'd arrogantly planned a tactical seduction, he thought, he was really off his game.

Why did he have to keep reminding himself that the easy charms that always worked with other women wouldn't work with Ruby? He gave a low, rueful laugh.

She looked discomfited. "What's so funny?"

"I'll send it all back." Coming closer to her, he pulled her into his arms. "And I'll arrange college tuition for Ivy. As for the rest, have I not made it clear enough that you should never worry about money again?"

"But—"

"I mean it, Ruby." His voice held an edge. "You insult me with your worry. You insult my very honor as a man. I will provide for you."

She stared at him, then muttered ungraciously, "Fine."

With a deep breath, he gentled his tone. "Later this afternoon, I've made you an appointment with the best obstetrician in New York."

Her eyes went wide. "You did?"

"If you're up to it. If you're not, I can reschedule."

"What time?"

"We'd need to leave at one thirty."

"I…I think that's all right."

"Then I'll leave you to rest." He pointed toward the intercom. "If you get hungry or need anything at all, press that button and Mrs. Ford will assist you." He tilted his head. "Would you care to join me for lunch downstairs at noon?"

She gave him a crooked smile. "In that huge formal dining room?"

"Try it." His lips curved. "You might like it."

Her dark eyes were huge in her beautiful face. Her teeth bit into her pink, delectable lower lip. Suddenly, all he wanted to do was take her in his arms. His blood was raging for him to kiss her. And more. He'd wanted her for too long. Having her so close, in his house, alone with him in this bedroom, he wanted her so badly he shook with it. The bed was right there.

"All right," she whispered. "Lunch."

It took all Ares's willpower to leave her bedroom, closing the door behind him. For a moment, he stood in the hallway, staring at the door. Then he forced himself to turn away. He hoped Ruby would enjoy her bubble bath.

As for him, he'd be taking his shower cold.

It was ten minutes past noon when Ruby rushed down the hallway in a panic. In spite of Ares's earlier tour, she'd still managed to get lost twice on her way to the dining room. And she was already late.

After a nervous night tossing and turning on his private jet, racked by fitful, sensual dreams of him that left her shivering with desire, Ruby had taken a long, leisurely bath, then fallen asleep as soon as her head hit the pillow. She'd woken to discover it was already past noon.

With nothing clean to wear, she'd grabbed lacy undergarments and a black shift dress out of the closet in desperation. But one swift glance to the mirror had told her the elegant dress made her skin look ashy, with a boxy cut that made her shapeless and wide, instead of pregnant. New leather sandals felt tight on her feet, and she'd been scared to even touch the Hermès bags. Her old floral canvas bag hung on her shoulder.

Her heart was pounding as she looked for the dining room in increasing panic. She was late, later by the second, which was so rude, and all because she couldn't even find the stupid dining room in this hideously huge mansion that went on forever and had too many hallways that looked exactly the same and...

"Ruby," his voice called gruffly.

Relieved, she turned and saw Ares through a doorway, sitting at the large antique table. She went into the dining room with a sigh. "I'm so sorry I'm late."

Ares set down his newspaper with a smile, which froze when he saw the shapeless dress. He recovered quickly. "I trust you had a good rest?"

"Yes, thank you." Flinching, she waited for him to make some comment about how she looked, probably using words like *shapeless* and *sack*. She couldn't blame him. How could she, when she'd been so honest about not liking his house?

He motioned toward a side table. "I guessed you'd prefer to serve yourself rather than having Mrs. Ford wait on us."

Ruby brightened when she saw the huge buffet in warming trays—eggs, bacon, waffles, fruit and fried potatoes, and baked chicken, buttered vegetables in herbs, freshly baked bread and creamy pasta carbonara. "Breakfast *and* lunch?"

"I wasn't sure what you'd want, so I asked Mrs. Ford to make a few things. You are pleased?"

"It's like a dream!" But as she grabbed a plate, she hesitated, feeling guilty. "But I don't need so much. What will happen to all the food that's left?"

"What do you mean?"

"It won't go in the trash, will it?" Biting her lip, she remembered the times her family had struggled to buy groceries at the end of the month. "Someone will get to eat it, right?"

His dark eyes focused on her abruptly. "I'll offer any leftovers to my staff. Mrs. Ford is an excellent cook so I expect it will disappear. And I'll instruct Dorothy to make an immediate donation to the local food bank."

Ruby beamed at him, then filled her plate with a bit of everything, until food was piled recklessly high on the elegant twenty-four-karat-gold-edged china plate. Pouring herself a glass of frothy, freshly squeezed orange juice, she carried them toward the table, then plunked down in the seat next to him. "Thank you! This is amazing!"

He smiled at her warmly. "I'm glad you approve."

Beneath his glance, her cheeks went pink as her body flooded with sensual awareness. Turning away, she focused on her food. Each bite was more delicious than the last.

"Mrs. Ford can really cook," she said, though as her mouth was full, it sounded like "Mmph. Fwmph cahwee coo."

Luckily Ares understood. Taking a gulp of coffee and a bite of his own plain eggs and bacon, he gave a low laugh. "Yes, she can."

"Mmm" was all she could spare as an answer. She felt like she hadn't eaten in days.

She was almost shocked when she heard the tines of her fork scrape against the china. She looked at the empty plate, then lifted her shocked gaze to his. "I ate the whole plate."

"Take more. Take whatever you want." His dark eyes lingered over her, traveling from her plate, to her hands, to her breasts and finally her eyes. He said huskily, "Take everything."

He looked at her, then deliberately at the stately oak table. As if he were thinking he'd like to shove the plates and silverware and vase of flowers to the floor, rip the shapeless dress off her, tip her back on the table and explore every sensitive curve of her naked, pregnant body.

There was a loud clatter. She realized she'd dropped her fork.

Trembling, she took a deep breath as she picked it up. She'd made a mistake. She shouldn't have sat in the chair next to his. He was too close. Her gaze fell to his forearms, laced with dark hair below his rolled-up sleeves. His powerful thighs, thick with muscle beneath well-tailored black trousers, were just inches from hers.

Pushing her hands against the table, Ruby rose unsteadily to her feet. "We're going to be late."

Tilting his head, he leaned back in his chair and gave her a lazy grin, as if he knew exactly what she was worried about. "Dr. Green will wait for us."

Her eyebrows lifted skeptically. "You said she was the best obstetrician in the city. No way she will just *wait*."

"She will for us, since in exchange for caring for you, I offered to completely fund her charitable foundation for two years."

"Oh," said Ruby. Her own attempts at sweet-talking people usually involved a plate of her sister's home-baked cookies, not funding some foundation for probably millions of dollars. She lifted her chin desperately. "Still. That's no excuse to be rude."

Glancing at his platinum watch, Ares said, "You're right." He abruptly rose from the breakfast table, tossing down his napkin. "I'll ask Horace to bring around the car."

Placing his hand gently on the small of her back, he led her from the dining room. Trembling, she moved away from his hand. And tried to act like she didn't still burn where he'd touched her.

CHAPTER SEVEN

"THE BABY LOOKS HEALTHY. The pregnancy is progressing just fine." The obstetrician's smiling face looked between them questioningly. "Do you want to know whether it's a boy or a girl?"

Sitting on the examination chair of the sleekly modern medical clinic, Ruby exclaimed, "Yes!" at the same moment Ares said firmly, "No."

Dr. Green's rosy expression didn't change as she held the ultrasound wand over Ruby's belly. "Well, which?"

"Of course we want to know." Ruby frowned at Ares. "Why wouldn't we want to know?"

Ares looked back at her, feeling a little sick. He'd never imagined taking her to the doctor could be so difficult. His shoulders were tight, his hands clenched at his sides. He felt painfully tense. And he wasn't even the patient. All he'd done was sit beside her. And learn about the pregnancy.

He didn't want to know if the baby was a boy or a girl. It was bad enough that he'd already been forced to hear the heartbeat. So rapid, so *real*. He didn't want this child made more real to him. Not when he knew that his only connection after the birth would involve his DNA and his money.

But he could hardly explain that to Ruby. Or even fully explain to himself why it was bothering him so much. His body was reacting as if he were under attack.

"I want to know if it's a boy or girl," Ruby said.

Ares blinked. "I…would rather be surprised."

"How about Dr. Green just tells me? I'll keep it a secret from you, I promise!"

Ruby looked so hopeful. Ares glanced at the doctor, hoping she would smooth things over. Dr. Green, who was no fool, just smiled. "I'll leave you two to discuss it."

But as the doctor rose to her feet, Ares knew that he didn't want to be left alone to discuss it with Ruby. "Fine. Have it your way."

Ruby's beautiful face filled with delight. "Really?"

He had to find out sometime, didn't he? His jaw clenched. "Might as well get it over with." He looked at Dr. Green. "Go ahead."

The doctor paused, looking between them. "Very well." Then she sat back down in front of the ultrasound screen. Pointing out lines and shapes that seemed like a blur, she beamed at them. "Congratulations. You're having a girl."

A girl.

With those words, against his will, Ares could picture a child—a little girl with her mother's big dark eyes and kind heart. So young. So fragile. He would need to protect her, as he protected her mother. He'd teach her to be strong. To fight. And most of all, how to lead. It would be necessary when someday she would take over his company and...

Ares stopped the thought cold. He thought he had anything to teach a child? He thought he could actually have the character, the experience, to make a good father?

Nice joke, he mocked himself cruelly.

Once the doctor left them, as Ruby started to change out of the patient gown and back into her black dress, Ares turned and fled the exam room door, racing down the end of the hall like a competitive sprinter.

Once he was out of the medical clinic, out into the hot, humid August afternoon, he took a deep breath, leaning forward with his hands against his knees. People hurried past him on the sidewalk, staring at him, giving him wide berth. He felt dizzy, his heart pounding.

Ares thought a visit to the doctor's office would make him feel more in control of their future. He was accustomed to being in charge of everything and everyone. He was accustomed to barking orders that the people around him, whether they worked for him or not, trembled and obeyed.

But he could not control this. Ruby had conceived his child, and when the baby was born, she would return to Star Valley, and he'd rarely see them. He would teach his daughter nothing. He would not protect her, except financially. His daughter would grow up knowing Ares only as a distant figure who paid the bills. Ruby would fall in love with another man someday and marry him. That unknown man, whoever he might be, would be his daughter's real father. And Ruby's husband for life.

The thought made him sick. But he could not change it. He'd be no good as a husband or father. Those roles involved qualities he did not have, like the ability to love, and to put his wife's and child's needs ahead of his own.

It's for the best, he told himself harshly. *Forget it. It doesn't matter.*

Ruby caught up with him on the sidewalk just as he waved down Horace, who brought the Rolls-Royce to the curb of the busy Midtown street.

"Where's the fire?" she demanded, sounding hurt. "Why did you rush out so fast?"

"Did I?" he said flatly.

"I had to wait for a new prescription for prenatal vitamins, and make my next appointment. I didn't know when you'd be able to come, so..."

"Next time you're going alone." He opened the passenger door before the sedan had even come to a full stop. "Get in."

"You don't want to come to doctor appointments?" Ruby said wistfully as she climbed in.

"I have a company to run." Getting in beside her, he leaned forward and gave Horace the name of a designer store on Fifth Avenue. He turned to her with a smile so forced, it strained his face. "Now I'm taking you shopping. You didn't like the other clothes. We'll get you new ones. Plus, you need a ball gown and jewelry. Perhaps a diamond necklace? A tiara like a princess?"

As he feared, Ruby was not so easily distracted.

"Why are you acting so weird?" she said as the sedan merged into traffic.

He glared at her. "I am not acting weird."

"What's wrong?"

"Nothing."

"Are you disappointed it's a girl?"

"That's the most ridiculous thing you've ever said to me."

"Then why?"

He turned to her. "I want the baby to have my last name. Even though we're not wed. Do you agree?"

"Why?" she asked, visibly taken aback.

"Is it so strange for a child to have her father's name?"

"No," she said slowly. "I guess not. But it will be a pain filling out forms, with my last name different from hers. Ivy and I liked having the same name as our mom. So even strangers knew we were a family."

"I have no family," he said slowly. "I am the last Kourakis."

Silence fell as they drove down Fifth Avenue. Ruby gave him an encouraging smile. "Of course she can have your name. It will be fine. Lots of families have different names, don't they? And it all works out."

"Thank you," he said quietly.

Looking out her window at the crowded sidewalks, she murmured, "So many people."

"Tourists."

"I would love to be a tourist. See the Statue of Liberty and Times Square and all that stuff."

He stared at her. "Are you kidding?"

"No. You might have lived here a million years but I haven't. And after I go back to Star Valley," she added wistfully, "I don't know if I'll ever be back."

"Fighting the crowds through Times Square on a hot, humid August day is my idea of hell."

"I guess we could wait till the weather's better. The baby's not due till Christmas…"

He flinched. "Christmas is worse. The Thanksgiving parade starts the whole ridiculous season. Rockettes in tiny elf hats. Santas ringing bells at every corner, begging for donations."

Her lips lifted on the edges. "How about October, then?"

Setting his jaw, he said nothing. She just stared at him, until he finally bit out, "What?"

"I'm just waiting for you to tell me what you hate about October in New York."

She was secretly amused, he realized. The harder he tried to repress his irritation, the more it seemed to bleed out of him. And rather than snapping back in her turn, Ruby was just watching him, as if trying to understand the reason for his bad mood. Which was even worse.

Clearing his throat, he changed the subject. "You haven't asked me why you need a ball gown."

"Why do I need a ball gown?" She gave him a crooked smile. "Don't tell me you're actually going to use that ballroom of yours?"

He shook his head. "We're attending a charity gala tomorrow night."

She shrank a little into the smooth leather seat. *"We?"*

"It is a big society event. I ordered a table. My ex-girlfriend backed me into a corner, but I think she's afraid a summer gala might have trouble attracting big-name donors."

"You want me to attend a big society event?" Ruby now looked horrified. "And it's hosted by your ex?"

"Is that a problem?" he said coolly, as if she were being unreasonable to object.

"Yes!"

"I know these kind of events can be tedious…"

"*Tedious* isn't exactly the word I'm thinking!"

"But I thought, if I took you out shopping for a designer ball gown and extravagant—truly extravagant—jewels, it might take out the sting."

She set her jaw. "So you're trying to bribe me?"

"If you want to call it that. I could have already arranged for the ball gown, but I thought you might enjoy picking it out."

Ruby folded her arms. "I don't need a fancy ball gown. Or jewels."

He blinked. "You don't want jewels?"

"I'd feel embarrassed wearing something so expensive when the fake diamonds look just as good. Especially when so many people are in need…"

"It's a charity ball for children," he interrupted. "All the proceeds go to them."

Ruby looked a little discomfited. "Which charity?"

He wished he'd listened when Dorothy had tried to tell him. "A good one."

She waited.

"It…um…helps kids in need," he finished, then demanded arrogantly, "You wouldn't turn your back on those kids, would you?"

She bit her lip. "I guess not. But I don't need an expensive ball gown," she added quickly. "That would be such a waste of money. Please donate the amount you would have spent on it directly to the charity."

Ares felt at a loss.

"Then, what will you wear tomorrow?" he said acidly. "Do you plan to attend naked?"

"Darn. I guess I can't go," Ruby said, looking sorrowful in a way that he didn't believe for a second. She brightened. "But at least I still helped the kids with the ball gown money. So it's kind of a wash, don't you think?"

Ares had no intention of going to the gala alone. He knew the glamour and romance of the evening would be too overwhelming for any woman to resist, even Ruby.

He pulled out his phone. "I have a better idea."

Twenty minutes later, the sedan was pulling into a little street in the Meatpacking District, not too far from the High Line.

"Where are we going?" Ruby asked for the third time.

And for the third time, Ares replied smugly, "It's a surprise."

She sighed.

"I hate surprises," she grumbled.

"Why?"

"They're never things like chocolate cake or winning lottery tickets, in my experience. It's always stuff like unexpected bills, or your car breaks down, or you slip on ice and break your ankle. Surprises are the worst."

He gave her a mischievous grin. "Wait and see."

The sedan stopped, and Horace opened their door. They were outside an enormous, old-looking warehouse. The concrete walls were covered with the peeling paint of old advertisements that looked decades old.

Ruby tilted back her head. Her voice sounded breathless as she said, "What is this place?"

Ares just hoped this would work. Taking her hand, he led her through the door.

Inside, the warehouse was huge, with high ceilings, filled with light and color, and with racks and racks of vintage clothes from every decade. Ruby gasped, craning her neck to look in every direction, at all the interesting clothes, and the even more interesting people shopping there.

Funky music played over the speakers. They were greeted by a smiling fortysomething woman with fuchsia hair. "Welcome." Her eyes popped behind her horn-rimmed glasses. "Excuse me, but are you...Ares Kourakis?"

"I am." He looked around. "And this is the best vintage clothing shop in Manhattan?"

The woman nearly dropped the plate of pink cupcakes she was holding. "Yes! At least I think it is."

"The internet agrees with you. That's why we're here." He looked over at Ruby. "My...friend needs a ball gown. And a whole new wardrobe, in fact."

"I'll help her myself," the pink-haired woman said eagerly. "But first... Won't you have one?" She held the tray out to Ruby.

"I've never seen anyplace like this," she breathed as she took a cupcake.

The other woman replied with a grin, "We have to compete with online retailers and can't do it on price. So we make it an *experience*."

"And you said surprises never involved cake," Ares murmured to Ruby as they followed the fuchsia-haired woman toward the racks of bright vintage clothes.

Ruby smiled at him, her eyes shining as she bit into the pink-frosted cupcake. "I've never been more happy to be wrong."

Funny, Ruby thought. She'd been so scared of coming to New York, she wouldn't have done it, if Ares hadn't forced her. But her first day here had already been one of the best days of her life.

She'd gotten to hear her baby's heartbeat, and found out that she'd be having a little girl.

Ruby still didn't understand Ares's weird reaction after the ultrasound. She'd been hurt at first. Then he'd asked that the baby take his last name. It was sweet, really. Maybe he just hadn't known how to express his emotions, she thought. But actions mattered more than words.

She loved that he'd brought her to a vintage shop, instead of a fancy department store.

The huge vintage warehouse had been a revelation. Ruby had never seen anything like it. Clothes from every decade, of every size and color, all housed together.

Looking around, she'd realized that the customers were like that, too. She smiled at babies in strollers wearing 1980s dresses and old seersucker suits, and an elderly woman in a vintage Chanel jacket pushing a bright green walker tricked out with rhinestones.

How could Ruby have been so scared of coming to New York City? These were her people. They were just like the folks she loved at home.

Maybe people were people, she thought, no matter where you happened to be.

"How did you create this place?" she'd breathed

to the pink-haired woman helping her navigate the aisles, who turned out to be the owner.

Wanda had laughed. "How do you start anything? By being brave and jumping in."

Those words rang in Ruby's ears as she spent hours pleasurably going through the racks, selecting maternity clothes for herself and a few things for their coming baby. At the end, the entire cost of her new wardrobe, ball gown included, had been under three hundred dollars.

Ares had nearly choked when he'd heard the amount at the cash register. He kept asking Wanda how she could expect to make a profit, and repeating that he didn't need a special discount. She'd assured him she was charging regular prices, but Ares still looked uncomfortable. Right before they left the shop, Ruby had seen him surreptitiously stick a bunch of hundred-dollar bills into the old painted mason jar marked "Cupcake Donations."

As they climbed into the waiting sedan, with Horace packing all the shopping bags into the trunk, Ruby leaned back against the back seat with a satisfied sigh. She looked up at Ares as he got in beside her.

Reaching out, she took his hand in her own.

"Thank you," she whispered.

He looked down at her hand wrapped over his. He slowly lifted his dark eyes to hers.

Electricity crackled between them, and his gaze fell to her mouth.

A shiver went through her. Against her will, she licked her lips. She heard his intake of breath. Deliberately, he lowered his head toward hers.

At the last moment, she turned away before he could kiss her, ripping her hand from his.

She said in a small voice, "I can't."

"Why?" he demanded.

"Because…" She glanced unwillingly toward Horace, who'd just sat down in front of the wheel. She bit her lip.

"Because we're not alone?" Ares said.

"I don't see anything, ma'am," Horace said from the front as he drove the sedan back onto the street.

Ruby gave a choked laugh, then said softly, "It's not just that. I…" She paused, then finally shook her head. "Never mind."

"Tell me," Ares whispered, twisting a long dark tendril of her hair around his finger. As she met his gaze, her lips burned with the tantalizing memory of his kiss.

"I'm the mother of your baby," she said haltingly.

"And perhaps, someday, your...friend. But that's all it can ever be."

"Why?" he growled.

"I told you. I'm never going to be that stupidly reckless again."

"You think I would hurt you?"

She looked down, refusing to answer.

They drove in silence. It was rush hour, and traffic was appallingly slow. She could feel his gaze on her, even as she woodenly stared out at the passing city.

"Are you hungry?" he said finally.

That made her look up with a faint smile. "I'm always hungry."

Leaning forward, he abruptly told Horace, "Pierre's."

Forty minutes later, Ruby and Ares were walking into a wood-paneled, elegantly rustic French restaurant. Though the place was packed with glamorous diners, they had no difficulties about a reservation. When Ares walked in, the maître d' looked delighted and immediately started fawning over him in fluent French. Ruby was astonished when Ares answered him in the same language.

Within moments, the two of them were sliding into a prime table by the window. After the drinks had been chosen and poured, when they were finally alone at the elegant, candlelit table, Ruby asked, sipping her sparkling water, "You speak French?"

Ares shrugged. "My mother lived in Paris for many years. I went to boarding school in Switzerland when I was eight."

Her eyes widened. "Your parents sent you away from home at eight?"

"It was a blessing," he said shortly. "I was glad to be away from them. And I attended some of the best schools in the world, in Switzerland and in America." He took a measured sip of his red wine. "My childhood prepared me for the life I live now. And my parents, for all their faults, did teach me one thing." Setting down his glass, he looked at her. "How to fight without remorse or mercy."

She stared at him in shock. "That's a horrible thing to learn from your own family."

"But valuable. It prepared me for the real world." He reached over the table, putting his hand over hers. "In the real world, you either win or lose. With family, that's truest of all."

His touch caused prickles through Ruby's body. She pulled her hand away. "That's all wrong."

"Is it?" Smiling humorlessly, he picked up the

menu. "You took care of your sister from child-hood, and she still cut you out of her life the instant you took something she wanted. Something that was never a possibility for her in the first place."

Ruby bit her lip. "I wouldn't say she cut me out, exactly..."

"I assume you've tried to contact her since we left Star Valley."

"Yes."

"Has she answered any of your messages?"

Compulsively, Ruby checked her phone, which she'd done a thousand times in the last two days. A lump rose in her throat. "No."

Ares took another sip of his wine. "She will. Soon."

"How do you know?"

"I've instructed my executive assistant to arrange payment for Ivy's tuition and a monthly stipend if she enrolls in college."

Her heart twisted. Just thinking of Ivy made her homesick and sad. "You think that will make her forgive me?"

He gave a cynical smile. "Absolutely."

"You can't buy everything," she whispered, thinking of her fear that he would soon own her, as well.

"Anything money cannot solve I do not want."

"Because you don't do complicated."

"Correct."

She took a deep breath, then met his gaze.

"That's why I can't let you kiss me," she whispered. "Because I'm afraid you'll break my heart."

For a moment, Ares stared at her, his handsome face shocked. Then he said in a low voice, "So leave your heart out of it. What does love have to do with sex?"

Now Ruby was the one to be shocked. "Everything."

"That belief will cause you to lose out on a great deal of pleasure, and gain you a great deal of pain," he observed, then turned to the menu. "Do you prefer lamb or veal?"

Two hours later, as they climbed back into the waiting sedan, Ruby greeted their long-suffering driver with a tentative smile. She thrust a brown bag emblazoned with *Pierre's* into his hands.

"What's this?" Horace said in surprise.

"You've been so patient, driving us around all day," Ruby said. "I thought you might be hungry."

Frowning, Horace glanced at his employer.

"Don't look at me," Ares said. "It was all her idea."

"I ordered you a *croque monsieur*. It's a toasted ham and cheese. You'll like it."

"It's what Ruby liked," Ares observed, "instead of *blanquette de veau*."

She wrinkled her nose. "That was not good."

"Or the *pâté de fois de lapin*."

"Yuck! I'm not eating the squashed liver of some poor rabbit!" She brightened as she turned to their driver. "But you'll like this. I ordered it right before we left. It should still be hot."

"Thank you, Miss Prescott," Horace said.

"Ruby."

"Ruby," the driver acknowledged, smiling.

She felt happy about that, at least, as they drove back to the Upper East Side. But there was a great deal she did not feel happy about.

She never should have told Ares the truth about why she couldn't let him kiss her. Their conversation afterward had been stilted and awkward. She'd tried to fill the silence by talking about possible names for their coming baby. That had gone over like a ton of bricks.

It filled Ruby's heart with despair. When Ares insisted on giving the baby his surname, she'd hoped he might be reconsidering his position on fatherhood. But now he didn't want to talk about their baby at all. Was he really so uninterested in their child? Could he truly offer nothing but money?

As they drove north on Third Avenue, a heavy silence stretched between them. Ruby felt hemmed in by tall buildings on every side. She couldn't see the horizon, or hear the soft sigh of the wind through the cottonwood trees. Instead, there was a crush of people, of cars, of sirens and horns.

Once the baby was born, she'd go home, she promised herself. *Home.* Just thinking of Star Valley made her homesick. She missed Ivy.

Finally, she could take the silence no longer.

"Ares." She turned to him in the back seat. "Can I ask you something?"

"If you want to ask, just do it."

"Why do you hate your parents so much?"

His jaw tightened, and he looked away. "I don't hate them."

"You said you were happier after they died."

"It's complicated."

"You don't do complicated."

"They're why." His expression was hard as he looked at her. "My parents hated each other, and dragged me constantly into their war. My mother never wanted to marry my father. Her parents forced her into it, though she was in love with someone else."

"How could they?"

He shrugged. "In society families, it's not uncommon. Power and money make a marriage. So whenever my father was unfaithful, which was often, my mother taunted him, hinting I might not be his son. I looked just like him, so he told her she was a filthy liar. It was only at my father's funeral that she finally admitted to me that I was his son. She'd hated him so much, she just wanted him to suffer."

"Oh, no."

Ares's lips twisted sardonically. "My mother hated me, too. I'd trapped her permanently into a marriage she'd never wanted, with a man she despised. A man who humiliated her for sport."

Pain radiated from Ruby's heart. She couldn't imagine growing up like that. Her father had abandoned her before she was born, and her family had always been on the wrong side of broke. But at least she'd never once doubted the fierce intensity of her mother's love for her and Ivy. "I'm so sorry…"

"A year later, she died as well, heli-skiing in Patagonia with her latest boy toy." His voice was cold. "I felt nothing but relief. All I ever was to them was a weapon. A burden. Never a son."

Ruby's heart was breaking. "Oh, Ares…"

He turned on her fiercely. "Our baby's childhood will be different. We will put our daughter's needs above our own selfish desires. We won't fight."

"Of course we won't," Ruby said comfortingly.

"I know." His dark eyes were like ice. "Because you will be raising her without me."

He'd said that before, but hearing him say it now, after he'd actually heard their baby's heartbeat, Ruby felt like she'd been punched. "But—just because your parents were like that, it's no reason—"

"I know my limitations," Ares said flatly. "I know who I am. And who I'm not." He looked away. "But as I said. She'll always be provided for. So will you."

Licking her lips, she said, "But you've never had a child before. How do you know you can't be a good father?"

"Because I know."

Her heart hurt. The more she got to know him, the more she wished things could be different. That he could be different. Her baby didn't just need financial support, but a flesh-and-blood father.

Ruby tried to smile.

"Try it. You might like it," she said wistfully, echoing his earlier words.

Ares stared at her as the sedan pulled to the curb in front of his nineteenth-century mansion. Horace leaped out to open her door, then started pulling shopping bags from the trunk. Ruby went back to help, ignoring his protests. As she turned back toward the house carrying bags, she saw Ares was still in the car. Frowning, she looked into the back seat.

"Aren't you coming?"

"You go ahead," he said. "I need to go to the office."

"But it's—" she swiftly consulted her phone "—almost ten at night!"

"Yes," he said crisply. "And I've been away from it too long. The company won't run without me. Horace?"

Handing her the rest of the bags, the driver looked at her sympathetically. "Ring the doorbell. Mrs. Ford will let you in. I'll wait until she does."

Bewildered, Ruby went up the steps to the elegant limestone mansion and rang the doorbell. A few moments later, the housekeeper answered.

"I trust you had a good evening, madam," she said icily.

"I…um…" Ruby looked behind her just in time to see the Rolls-Royce driving away. A lump rose in her throat. "Yes," she whispered. "And no." And carrying her bags of beautiful vintage clothes and broken dreams, she went inside.

CHAPTER EIGHT

IT HAD BEEN a mistake.

A catastrophic mistake.

Ares could see that now.

He never should have brought Ruby to New York. Never installed her in his house. Never gone with her to the doctor, or taken her to that vintage boutique.

Then he would never have had to see her face light up with joy. Her gaze wouldn't have pierced his heart as they heard their baby's heartbeat. He never would have shared memories about his parents, or heard Ruby's voice tremble as she asked him questions like *How do you know you can't be a good father? Try it. You might like it.*

Ares sat alone at the long dining table the next morning, across from the huge Ming vase filled with fresh flowers. He took a long drink of black coffee. The hot beverage burned his throat. Setting down his newspaper, he stared bleakly out the window overlooking the leafy street.

He had stayed at the office past midnight last night, talking to lawyers. He hadn't come home until he was sure Ruby would be asleep. He hadn't wanted to face any more questions.

For months now, he'd ached to feel her naked body back in his arms. But now, when he knew he was close to getting what he wanted—just the look in her eyes when he'd taken her to the vintage boutique had told him that—he was afraid.

Ruby was dangerous. She had a way of getting past his defenses. Of making him feel things he shouldn't feel. Want things he shouldn't want.

She almost made him wish he could be a different man.

But Ares couldn't change his character. He couldn't change what he knew to be true.

Love was a weapon. And he wouldn't let himself be annihilated by it ever again.

He never should have brought Ruby here.

He needed to send her away.

His lawyers were already drawing up the paperwork and expected to have it finished by late tonight. By tomorrow, Ruby would be on his private jet, headed back home, where she would raise their child as a single mother—and become one of the richest full-time residents of Star Valley.

Ares slammed his coffee cup against the wooden table.

Today would be their last day. Tonight their last night. He took a deep breath. He would use this time well. He'd romance her. Seduce her. Take as much of her as he could.

Because tomorrow she'd be out of his reach.

It's better this way, he told himself harshly. *Better for her. Better for me.*

"Good morning." Ruby entered the dining room, smiling at him shyly.

"I trust you slept well." He stood up courteously, even as a very uncivilized heat flooded through his body.

Ruby was wearing a 1950s-style red dress, with ties at the shoulders and a flirty skirt over her baby bump. Her dark hair flowed over her shoulders, her heart-shaped lips were scarlet and her brown eyes shone beneath black lashes as she looked at him. "I wasn't sure if I'd see you this morning. I thought you might have already gone to work."

"I'm taking today off."

"Those are your casual clothes?" Her lips lifted humorously at his long-sleeved black shirt and tailored black trousers. "Don't you own any shorts? It's supposed to get really hot."

"Shorts aren't my thing." His eyes traced over her hungrily. "You look beautiful."

"Oh. Thank you." Her cheeks went hot beneath his gaze. She quickly turned to the side table. "Wow. Mrs. Ford outdid herself again."

As Ruby loaded waffles, fruit and scrambled eggs on her plate from the chafing dishes, Ares's eyes traced over her long legs that ended in dark strappy sandals, her bare shoulders, her full breasts and the hint of a baby bump beneath the red skirt.

"I'm taking you to see New York today."

She turned to him, her eyes big. Then she smiled. "You mean you're sending one of your staff to take me around."

"No. I'm taking you."

She blinked. "But you said that touring New York in August is hell."

Ares thought of how he'd hungered for Ruby for nearly five months. How he hadn't been able to touch any other woman, because he'd wanted only her. That was the real hell. "I changed my mind."

Her lovely face lit up, and it was like sunshine after a rainstorm. "Yeah?"

"What do you want to see first? The Statue of Liberty? Times Square?"

"Oh, yes," she said eagerly. "And the museum."

"Art?"

"Dinosaurs." Setting her plate down on the table, she clapped her hands with the joy of a child. "I want to eat a hot dog from a cart. And a cannoli from Little Italy." She tilted her head. "What exactly *is* a cannoli, anyway?"

"Dessert."

"Is it any good?"

"You'll see," he said huskily.

Filling his own plate with plain toast, eggs and bacon, he returned to sit beside her.

Glancing up nervously, Ruby looked toward the end of the table with the folded newspaper. "I thought you were sitting down there."

"I was. Now I'm sitting with you."

Her cheeks went pink. She seemed careful not to let any part of her body touch his as she ate. He wondered if she was even tasting her breakfast.

He barely tasted his. He was impatient with food. It wasn't what he was hungry for.

As soon as her plate was empty, he said in a low voice, "Are you ready?"

"Oh, yes." She rose to her feet so quickly, she nearly lost her balance. "I didn't have any plans today, other than reorganizing the closet. And maybe seeing if I could help Mrs. Ford in the kitchen. Though she already made it plain she doesn't want my help." She gave a shy smile. "I was feeling kind of lonesome last night after you left, so I went into the kitchen to see if I could help tidy up. It's what I always have done, you see. Clean up. Mrs. Ford yelled at me that pregnant women need peace and rest and I was to go relax and get out of her kitchen. But we ended up sharing a pot of tea."

"A pot of tea? With Mrs. Ford?" Ares was astonished.

"Oh, yes." Leaning forward, Ruby confided, "I used to be intimidated by her. But not anymore. She's nice."

Nice? He'd never thought of his stiff-necked housekeeper that way. He wondered uneasily how long it would have been before Ruby's insights stretched into his soul, as well.

Well, that was why he was sending her away. Because she was dangerous to his peace of mind.

"Mrs. Ford promised to teach me how to play pinochle tomorrow," Ruby added with a grin. "Apparently she's quite a card shark. Belongs to a league and everything."

Pinochle league? This side of Mrs. Ford was news to him. But the lesson would never happen.

Because tomorrow Ruby would be gone. The thought caused a sharp feeling in his throat. He pushed it away grimly.

It's for her own good. And mine.

Forcing his face into a smile, he held out his arm. "Are you ready?"

Ruby hesitated, then tentatively wrapped her hand over his arm, clearly trying to keep her body as far away from his as possible. "If you are."

Ares looked down at her, aching with desire. Let tomorrow's problems wait. For now he had a whole day of her company—and a night.

Oh, yes. He was ready.

They started with a helicopter ride, of all things.

Ruby's eyes nearly popped out of her head as the Rolls-Royce dropped them at a small private heliport on the other side of the East River, behind a guarded gate. As she gawked around her, Ares led her past the small executive lounge to the tarmac, where she saw a waiting Sikorsky S-76 helicopter, emblazoned with *Kourakis Enterprises.*

Ruby flashed him a grin. "You put your name on everything, don't you?"

"Everything I care about," he said, then his jaw tightened and a strange look crossed his face.

She heard the loud noise of the helicopter's engine warming up. Two pilots were visible in the cockpit, waiting. She put her hands over her ears. Then she stopped completely, ten feet from the helicopter.

Ares frowned down at her. "What's wrong?"

"I—I'm a little nervous," she choked out, raising her voice to be heard over the noise. She tried to smile. "I know it's silly, but I've never…"

Putting his hands on her shoulders, Ares roughly pulled her against his body. Her hands fell to her sides as she was swept into his arms. She gave a soft gasp, her lips parting, as she looked up at his face.

Then he lowered his lips to hers.

His kiss was hungry. Savage. And all of the pent-up hunger she'd tried to deny, suddenly burst through Ruby like an out-of-control blaze.

Her hands lifted around his shoulders, drawing him down against her. With a low growl, he tightened his arms, tipping her back, deepening the embrace until she could think of nothing but the demands of his mouth and tongue against her own.

Her knees went weak as she was lost in desperate pleasure. Need for him thundered through her, begging for release, for more, harder, deeper...

Finally, Ares pulled back. His dark eyes pierced hers.

"You're not afraid of the helicopter," he said, and it was a command, not a question.

Dazed, blinking in the sunlight, Ruby realized she was still standing on the tarmac of the private heliport. She shook her head. Helicopter? Who cared about that?

Ares's hot eyes caressed her. "Come with me now."

With a deep breath, she took his outstretched hand. The helicopter was luxurious inside, with four white leather seats, two front and back, a flat-screen television and a small refrigerator. Handing her a headset, he smiled at her.

"I knew you wouldn't be afraid."

"No," she said, swallowing hard. At the moment, riding a helicopter was the last thing she was worried about.

Then they took off, and she gasped at the view, pressing her nose to the window as she saw the glorious Manhattan skyline from every angle. They flew south to the majestic Brooklyn Bridge and the Statue of Liberty in New York Harbor, circling north to Wall Street and One World Trade Center, the tallest building in the city. Continuing to Midtown, she saw the Empire State Building, Rockefeller Center and the Chrysler Building, with its distinctive curved art deco spire. She saw everything Ares had told her about Central Park was true. It did have indeed have twenty-six separate baseball fields—and a castle.

"What's it for?" she asked him over the headset. "The castle?"

"Nothing," he said with a grin. "It's just beautiful." His handsome face turned serious. "But not half as beautiful as you."

With an intake of breath, Ruby looked away. She was still shivering from his kiss. If he'd asked for permission, she would have refused. But he hadn't asked. He'd only taken.

And now she couldn't stop trembling. Her lips felt bruised, her nipples hard beneath her red dress. She wanted more. That was the worst part. *She wanted more…*

She was careful to keep her distance from him as they flew by Central Park. Luckily, there was a good deal of space between the luxurious white leather seats. She was careful not to meet his eyes as they flew over Harlem and the Bronx, and he pointed out Yankee Stadium. "We can only fly over it because there's no game today." Finally the helicopter circled around, returning them back to the heliport.

"Well, what did you think?" he asked, smiling as he helped her out of the helicopter. "The entire city in less than an hour. New York for the tourist in a hurry."

Ruby staggered a little on her feet. Because of the helicopter ride, she told herself firmly. Not the kiss. She put a steadying hand on her head. "Why am I in a hurry? Don't I have months to explore the city?"

The smile slid from Ares's face. His jaw tightened. She tried not to shiver as he placed his hand gently on the small of her back. "We have a lot to do today."

Horace was waiting to drive them. They took the elevator to the top of the Empire State Building, like in *Sleepless in Seattle*. They walked through Times Square and saw the chaotic frenzy of tourists mingling with people in strange costumes aggressively trying to earn a living by taking pictures for tips in the pedestrians-only square.

The August day was sticky hot, as promised. By

noon, Ruby could feel a sheen of sweat on her skin. But it wasn't only because of the summer sun.

It was Ares. The intensity of his gaze caressing her. The feel of his hand over hers. The memory of his kiss, tingling her lips, and the continual burn like a furnace of knowing his baby was growing inside her.

Ruby had never known heat like this before.

The two of them ate their way across the city, starting with hot dogs on the street—to Ruby's disappointment, they just tasted like regular hot dogs—cannoli in Little Italy—which turned out to be a thin fried pancake wrapped around a sweet cream center—and dim sum in Chinatown—a whole bunch of tasty things served off a cart, with tea.

As he talked with her, listened to her, laughed with her, Ruby should have slowly relaxed. But she didn't. She only got more tense.

Ares couldn't be charming like this. It wasn't right. It wasn't fair. Because she knew this funny, charming, romantic man was an illusion.

But he made her want to believe it was real. All of it.

When he acted like this, he made her dream against her will. To wonder what it would be like to love him. To have him love her back. To actually be a real family, the two of them with their daughter.

As the afternoon waned, he said, "It's time to get ready for the gala. I'm not sure we have time to stop at your museum."

"Oh, please," she wheedled. "It won't take me long to get ready later. We still have time."

"In my experience, women demand two hours."

"Two hours!" Ruby exclaimed. "Good heavens. I can get ready in ten minutes." At his skeptical look, she amended, "All right. Since it's a special occasion and I'll want a shower, twenty minutes. Thirty, tops."

"You're quite a woman," he observed in a low voice, stretching his arm along the seat behind her. She could feel the warmth of him, the strength and power, against her shoulders. A sudden shiver went through her as she weighed the possibility of him pulling her into his arms and kissing her senseless in the back seat. She jumped when he told Horace, "The natural history museum for Ruby."

"Yes, sir," he said with a grin.

The two of them went in through a private entrance, holding hands, bypassing the crowds and lines, since—of course—Ares was a donor and had connections. They did a speed tour, led by a kindly docent. But as Ruby oohed and aahed over the dinosaur bones, she was conscious all the while of Ares watching her.

As they left, she impulsively asked if she could buy a stuffed toy bear in the gift shop. He looked delighted. "Of course," he growled. "Buy the whole damn shop if you want."

"Oh, it's not for me." She gave him a smile. "It's for our baby girl."

The smile vanished from his face.

"As you wish," he said tightly. And though he paid for the toy, he wouldn't even look at it.

All Ruby's joy fled. As they walked back to the car, even the sun seemed a little less bright.

How could Ares be so unfeeling? It was as if he was trying to pretend there was no baby. But wasn't that the reason he'd brought Ruby to New York—so he could keep an eye on her throughout her pregnancy?

On the silent drive home, Ruby wanted to speak with him, but didn't know how. He was so distant looking, staring coldly out his window, his jaw hard enough to cut glass.

Once home, he headed upstairs, calling back to her roughly, "Be ready in thirty minutes."

Twenty-nine minutes later, she'd finished putting on her red lipstick, and looked at herself in the full-length mirror, smacking her lips in satisfaction. She'd dreaded the thought of this gala, of facing a bunch of snooty society people and, if that weren't enough, his ex-girlfriend, too.

But she suddenly wasn't scared. She was the one on Ares's arm and living in his house. The mother of his child. She wasn't scared anymore. Not even of his silence.

Everything was going to be all right. Her lips lifted. In fact, as she remembered the way he'd kissed her today, the way his eyes had caressed her as if he never wanted to let her go, she focused on that and pushed away his strangely cold reaction to their baby. She told herself that everything would be fine. In fact—she touched her lips dreamily— maybe everything, against all odds, could be better than fine.

Ares couldn't take his eyes off Ruby. He had never seen anything like her.

Nor, it seemed, had anyone else.

The modern art museum where the charity ball was being held was just two city blocks from his house, so Ruby had insisted on walking, as the night was fine. When they'd walked in together, all eyes—both men's and women's—had turned to stare.

Ares could not blame them. He'd done the same when he'd seen Ruby come down the stairs, looking incredibly beautiful with her long dark hair twisted up in a high braided bun, wearing a vintage gown from the 1980s, a one-shouldered pink taffeta dress with a short bubble skirt. And big fake pearls.

An older woman, one of society's most elegant doyennes, had looked at her in astonishment. "Who did your dress?"

"Gunne Sax," Ruby had replied seriously, without cracking a smile.

All throughout the evening, as they'd enjoyed an elegant dinner with Ares's friends and acquaintances at their twelve-seat table in a prime location, people had been curious about her, wanting to talk to her.

At first, Ares had been nervous for her. He knew his class of people too well, how they could smile politely as they stuck a sharp knife through your back. He'd grown up in this world. He was used to it. Their cruelty washed over him like a September drizzle. But Ruby—she was too open. She was too kind. They would devour her.

But to his surprise, she'd held her own. Her friendliness and lack of pretense quickly made her popular in a way he hadn't expected. And now, as he returned to her with a glass of nonalcoholic punch, his body grew taut beneath his tuxedo as he remembered how he'd felt kissing her by the helicopter just a few hours ago.

He'd been thinking of skipping the gala altogether and whisking her straight to bed when that museum stuffed bear had ruined everything. Reminding him of the baby. Of his failure as a father. Of his lack of a soul.

Because he knew every moment he spent seducing Ruby today, without telling he was sending her away tomorrow, she would see as a betrayal.

Guilt was an emotion he hadn't felt in a long time. He didn't like it.

But if not for that stupid stuffed bear, he might be pleasurably in bed with her right now, instead of at this damned party, watching other men fawn over her.

"Who is she?" asked one of his friends, Cristiano Moretti. The Italian hotel tycoon's eyes traced over her curiously. "She's the star of the party."

Ares bared his teeth in a smile, not liking the man even looking at Ruby. Though his friend had been off his game lately, he was a notorious womanizer. But if he punched Cristiano and every other man staring at her right now, Ares would be here all night.

He looked at her, standing on the edge of the dance floor, surrounded by people. A band was playing a mix of pop, jazz and big band music that perfectly suited the ascetic white space of the soaring modern art museum.

He needed to get Ruby home, he thought. To claim her for himself alone. He felt like he'd spent his life wanting her. There was only so much a man could take.

Going to Ruby, Ares handed her the punch. Her eyes lit up. "Oh, thank you."

"Having a good time?"

She gave him a grin. "I don't understand half of what people are talking to me about. Apparently nannies are hard to come by, and the circuit traveling from Art Basel to Monaco has all just gotten too, too tedious these days."

"Ah," he said, watching her drink the punch, pressing the cup against her full, rosy lips. His body stirred, as if it needed any further stirring.

"Ares?" As a song ended, a couple came off the dance floor. The woman, a tiny, very pretty blonde in a slim-cut gray dress, came forward eagerly, dragging her male companion behind her.

Ares's jaw tightened when he saw his ex-mistress, the hostess of the charity ball whom he'd mostly managed to avoid till now. "Hello, Poppy."

"Thank you for buying a table," she cooed. "Tonight has been such a success. But then, I've had so many successes lately." Ignoring Ruby, she stuck her left hand in Ares's face. "Did you hear I'm engaged?"

He glanced passively at the diamond ring. It was ostentatious and huge and there was no way the spiky-haired young man beside her had paid for it. "Congratulations."

"Thank you." Poppy flashed an adoring gaze at her date. "Angus just dropped out of NYU. He's too good for college—a pure musical genius!"

"He's a singer?"

"Drummer," she said.

The young man, who had tattoos on his neck and a permanent snarl on his lips, tugged on her sleeve. "Come on, baby. There's an open bar." But Poppy looked at Ruby.

"Who's this?" she said casually, as if a hundred people hadn't likely told her.

"I'm Ruby," she said with a warm smile.

"Ruby Prescott," Ares said. "We met in Star Valley after you left."

"Star Valley?" Poppy said, frowning, then she gave a fake laugh. "Ah. Some little waitress from the country?"

"I was a bartender, actually," said Ruby.

Poppy gave her a sweet smile. "I do hope New York's not too overwhelming for you. But don't worry. It won't last long." She looked at Ares fondly. "He gets bored so easily."

Deliberately, he took Ruby's hand. "It will last longer than you think, Poppy, since Ruby's pregnant with my baby."

The change that went over the heiress's face was almost comical. She looked at Ruby's belly beneath the hot pink taffeta, then flashed a crocodile smile.

"A waitress. Who got pregnant. How very lucky!"

"I was a bartender," Ruby corrected. "Plus some other things. A snowboarding instructor. A house cleaner. But not a waitress, at least not lately."

"*So* lucky." Tilting her head, Poppy said sweetly, "At least, I trust it was luck, and not something more perfidious. Oh, forgive me—" she put her hand to her mouth with mock embarrassment "—you probably don't know what that word means. *Perfidious*—"

"I know what it means," said Ruby.

"Oh?" The blonde's voice was musical.

Ruby tilted her head and matched her sweet tone. "It means right now you're kicking yourself that you didn't somehow manage to get pregnant by him first."

Ares hid a smile. One point to Ruby, he thought.

Poppy's eyes narrowed. Then, tilting her head, she cooed, "So. A baby. I presume this means you two will be getting married soon?"

Folding his arms, Ares scowled. "There's no need."

"No?" Poppy suddenly seemed much happier. "Oh, Ares, how can you bring the poor country girl to New York knocked up and not even marry her? What are you planning to do, put her up in some house somewhere, like you're ashamed of her?"

He glared at her, furious at the direction the conversation had taken. "I'm not in the least ashamed—"

"Oh?" Poppy turned sympathetically to Ruby. "So it's you, then. You don't want to marry him?"

Her hands fell to her sides uncertainly. "I hadn't really thought…"

"Oh, Ares." Poppy made a *tsk* sound. "You won't marry her? Even though she's having your baby? Of course *you* would find a lifetime commitment impossible. But you didn't realize that, did you, my dear?" She patted Ruby's shoulder. "I feel so bad for you. Ares, I'm surprised you'd be so needlessly cruel. Or maybe—" her lips twisted upward as she looked between them "—not so surprised. Good luck, my dear."

And she left, dragging her spiky-haired musician behind her.

Ares looked at Ruby. A moment before, she'd been glowing. Now her shoulders seemed small. Even the big pink taffeta bows on her right shoulder seemed to slump a little. She wouldn't meet his eyes.

"Forget her," he said roughly. Reaching out, he took her hand. "Dance with me."

"I don't dance," she said unhappily, but he ignored her, pulling her out onto the dance floor beneath an art installation of multicolored glass stretching in all directions across the ceiling. The band was playing a slow, sad ballad.

Pulling her in his arms, he swayed with her, relishing the feel of her curvaceous body against his own. "See? You do dance."

She didn't respond. Didn't meet his eyes. He had to place her hand against the lapel of his tuxedo jacket.

"Ruby," he said quietly. "Look at me."

When she finally obeyed, her dark eyes were sad, luminous with unshed tears.

It was like a punch through his gut. And Ares suddenly realized what he'd done.

He'd been so determined to fulfill his own selfish desires. His need to have her in his bed. To protect himself by sending her away.

He'd never cared about her. Her feelings. How his actions might affect her.

That's why I can't let you kiss me. Because I'm afraid you'll break my heart.

Could he seduce her without loving her? But what would it do to her when she woke up in his arms tomorrow and he told her that he never wanted to see her again? That it was already *planned*?

He suddenly couldn't do it.

As the music continued, he stopped dancing, leaving the two of them frozen on the dance floor as other couples swirled around them.

"This isn't going to work," he said roughly.

"What isn't?" she choked, blinking fast. A hard lump rose in his throat.

"You living here."

"Because of what she said?"

"Poppy was right," he said in a low voice. "I'm being cruel."

"You're going to send me away?" she whispered. Setting his jaw, he looked away.

Her voice was choked with tears. "I don't understand. I came here. I've done everything you demanded of me."

What could Ares say? *It's not you, it's me?* Tell her that he'd thought he could just have sex with her and send her away when he was done, but now he realized she was too dangerous to toy with? That he'd realized that she was a real person with feelings of her own?

"My lawyers are already drawing up legal documents for us to sign. I'm transferring my ski lodge in Star Valley to your name. I've created a trust fund for our daughter, along with ordering a generous amount of monthly support for you." He paused. "Tomorrow, after the papers are signed, I'm sending you home."

"Why didn't you tell me?" she whispered. He looked at her.

"Because I intended to seduce you tonight."

Ruby sucked in her breath, searching his gaze.

Then she looked away, clenching her jaw. Lifting her shoulder, she wiped her eyes against the taffeta bow. When she looked back at him, her eyes were cold.

"Thank you for proving me right," she said.

Ares's jaw set as he remembered her words.

I've seen what happens when a rich man gets bored with his promises. In a few days or weeks you'll change your mind and toss me back on the street.

So? That's exactly who I am, Ares told himself savagely. Why try to fight it? Why let himself be tempted to be different, when it could only lead to vulnerability and pain?

"You lied to me," she whispered. "I actually was starting to believe..."

Her voice trailed off. Turning, Ruby fled, leaving him standing alone amid the crowds of beautifully dressed people on the dance floor.

"Ruby!"

She didn't stop. Crowds parted magically for her, as they'd always parted for him. But it wasn't due to wealth and power. They parted for Ruby's light. For her brilliant beauty. The bright fuchsia of her dress was like a beacon flying through a sea of gray dresses and black tuxedos.

Setting his jaw, Ares went after her. As she burst out of the museum and into the warm summer night, she looked back and saw him behind her. Pulling off her strappy sandals, she started running on the sidewalk.

Barefoot, she was surprisingly fast. He followed grimly in his Italian leather shoes, getting surprised looks as he ran past people in his tuxedo. She'd always been athletic. He remembered her snowboarding past him on the mountain. She reached the mansion a full four seconds before he did.

"Ruby!"

"Stop following me," she bit out, heading up the sweeping staircase.

"We can share an elevator—"

"I'd rather die."

As Ares watched Ruby climb up the staircase, her shoulders drooping in the bright pink dress, he told himself to let her go. Her misery would be brief. Tomorrow, she would be wealthy beyond belief, heading back home. To have her baby. Someday, she'd find another man, one who would know how to care for them both.

But as Ares looked up the shadowy staircase

where Ruby had disappeared, every ounce of his body and soul recoiled at the thought.

Ruby was his woman.

He couldn't let her go.

She was his.

Taking the elevator, he reached the top floor before she did. And he saw why she'd taken the long route. She was crying. Her eyebrows lowered in a fury when she saw him outside her door.

"Leave me alone."

"You're crying."

She tossed her head. "Tears of happiness. I never wanted to come to New York. You blackmailed me into it. I'm happy to go home." She looked up defiantly. "I knew this would happen!"

Tears were streaming down her cheeks.

Ares pulled her into his arms, his fingers twining in a dark tendril that had escaped her high ballerina bun. "Ruby, you're driving me crazy," he said huskily. "From the moment I first saw you, I haven't been able to think of any other woman. You're the only one I've wanted. Only you."

He heard her intake of breath.

"Are you saying—" she lifted her luminous gaze to his "—you've been faithful to me all these months?"

Faithful. Ares hadn't thought of it that way. But now he realized it was true. "Yes. Which is why I brought you here. To force you to take care of yourself, yes. But also because I needed you in my bed."

She swallowed.

"Then, why?" she whispered. "If you want me so badly, why are you sending me away so soon?"

"Because you're dangerous."

"Dangerous?" she said in astonishment.

"I didn't want to care about you, but I do." Cupping her cheek, he said in a low voice, "You're different from any woman I've ever known. Which is why after tonight, I can never see you again…"

Tilting back her head, he ruthlessly lowered his mouth to hers.

For an instant, her hands pressed against his shoulders, as if to resist. But he would not let her deny what he knew they both wanted. His grip tightened on her, holding her fast. He deepened his kiss, plundering her lips, teasing her tongue with his own until he felt her sigh. Until he felt her surrender, the roundness of her breasts and belly and her petite body against his tuxedo.

The strappy sandals she'd been holding dropped to the floor. Recklessly, she started to kiss him back, holding him tight against her, as if she, too, had yearned for this, not just for months, but all her life.

Desire surged through him. For nearly half a year, he'd hungered only for this woman. Having her in his arms now felt like the waking fulfillment of a dream. His hands tangled in her hair, loosening the pins of her braids. As they kissed each other, her long, dark, lustrous hair cascaded to her shoulders like a veil.

Lifting her in his arms, he carried her into his bedroom. He was trembling with need. He wanted to possess her, to rip off their clothes, to fall back on the enormous bed and pull her down over him, to push himself inside her until they both screamed with ecstasy.

But he had to be gentle. She was pregnant. He had to treat her as she deserved.

His hands shook as he slowly lowered her to her feet. Never taking his eyes off her, he reached around her, unzipping her pink taffeta dress. When it dropped to the floor, he swallowed.

Her pregnant body was more lush than he'd ever imagined. She wasn't wearing a bra. His gaze fell to her naked, swollen breasts, to the soft curve of her belly above the lace panties clinging to her full hips.

She was magnificent.

She fell back against the bed, as if her knees had stopped supporting her.

Looking down at her, spread across the shadows of his enormous bed wearing only lace panties, he wanted to fling himself on her, to take her with a masculine roar of possession.

But he did not. He could not.

His eyes lingered on her swollen breasts, huge with enticing red, rosy peaks. He'd always thought she was impossible to resist. But now she was a goddess.

His hands shook with the effort of restraint as he pulled off his tuxedo jacket. His black tie and white shirt. After kicking off his shoes, he took off his tuxedo pants and silk boxers.

He was aching, raging with the clanging need to take her, take her now. As he climbed next to her in bed, his whole body strained with the effort of self-control as he gently turned her face toward his. Without touching any other part of her, he kissed her, long and deep. He kissed her until he saw her body rise.

Gently, he rolled over, pulling her on top of him.

Her full thighs stretched over his hips, his hard shaft pressed against the swell of her belly. As she leaned down to kiss him, her delicious breasts swept against his muscled chest. Lifting one full red nipple to his mouth, he suckled her until she gasped, closing her eyes in an expression of joy. Tilting her head back, she cried out as she climaxed with his mouth around her nipple. *Just from that.*

As he felt her soft, curvaceous body shake, he nearly did the same. Hearing her gasp with pleasure, he looked up at her beautiful face, holy with ecstasy.

Triumph surged through him. He'd made her explode. Just like that. Because Ruby was his.

She was his.

Spanning her hips with his hands, he lifted her. Her eyes were still closed and she was still gasping with pleasure as he lowered her slowly over his hard, thick shaft, filling her inch by inch.

It was the first time he'd been inside her without a condom. He gave a low, involuntary groan as blinding pleasure roared through him.

She murmured with pleasure, instinctively swaying her hips against him. Gripping his shoulders, she pushed against him, pulling him even deeper inside her.

The last vestiges of Ares's self-control fled.

As he finally possessed her after such long, aching need, he was lost in sensation, drowning beneath her waves. Forgetting all thought of restraint, he put his hands on her hips, guiding her, pushing into her, filling her to the hilt. Her fingernails laced into his shoulders, as she met his passion with her own. Just a few deep thrusts and she climaxed again, this time with a loud, fierce cry. When he heard that, he gasped, then exploded, spilling himself inside her with pleasure so intense he almost passed out.

She softly collapsed beside him on the bed. He heard the low wheeze of his own breath. He felt the damp warmth of her skin as she pressed her body against his. Eyes closed, he pulled her tenderly against his bare chest, wrapping his arms around her, softly stroking her in the moonlit bedroom.

His. Ruby was his.

Ares has never felt this way about any woman. And he knew, whatever he'd planned, however dangerous she might be, he couldn't let her go. Not yet.

"Stay with me," he whispered, and he felt her stiffen in his arms.

"I thought you wanted me to leave tomorrow," she said in a low voice. "What about all your reasons for sending me away?"

"I changed my mind," he said in a low voice, his arms tightening around her. "Please stay."

She still wouldn't look at him. "For how long?"

Leaning down, Ares kissed her temple, inhaling the sweet scent of her, like sunshine and joy.

"For as long as you want."

Twisting her head, Ruby looked back at him, her beautiful face half hidden in shadow. And then, with the edge of her cheek frosted by moonlight, she smiled up at him, eyes shining.

CHAPTER NINE

IT WAS DONE.

Ruby stood in their brand-new nursery, looking around her with joy in her heart. Room by room, with Ares's blessing, she'd redecorated his—*their*—house over the last seven weeks, adding color, making it comfortable. Making it home.

"You're sure you don't mind?" she'd asked in August.

He'd softly kissed her. "Whatever makes you want to stay, I want you to have."

And that had been that.

Over August and September, she'd replaced the mansion's sharp avant-garde furniture with soft, squishy couches that felt good to lounge in. Redecorating had been a joy for her. But this last project had been her favorite by far—turning the former guest room, the one next to the master bedroom, into their daughter's nursery.

Ruby rubbed her over-six-months-pregnant belly and looked around her with satisfaction. The walls were now painted a cheerful light pink. The black four-poster bed had been replaced with a white crib, and the stark metal chandelier, with those hideously hard edges, was now a sweet white chandelier with baby animals on it. The huge walk-in closet had been filled with soft baby clothes and tiny shoes, and the accessories island turned into a changing table. A rocking chair now sat beside the window, and the bedroom had been filled with children's books, and so many toys and stuffed animals, it was half library, half zoo.

Ruby gave a sigh of contentment.

Living together, she and Ares had fallen into a rhythm. Each morning, he left for his building in Midtown. She spent the day working on the house, taking care of herself and going to doctor's appointments. He often came home for dinner late. Twelve-hour days were typical for him, even on weekends.

"The downside of running a company," he'd told her. "Always working."

"It's not a downside for you," she accused. "You like it."

He'd given her a wicked grin, then kissed her and said huskily, "Not as much as I like coming home to you in my bed."

Ruby shivered, remembering. He always knew how to seduce her. He made her feel so good at night, making love to her in their hot, dark, deliciously sensual private paradise. Nighttime was her favorite time.

But during the day...

Ruby stopped the thought in its tracks.

She was fine, she told herself firmly. This city was becoming home to her. New York wasn't that different from Star Valley, she'd realized. No matter where you lived—in small towns or big cities— people were people.

She'd attended several galas and other events since that first charity ball. And though some of Ares's acquaintances, especially his former mistresses, had scorned her as Poppy Spencer had warned, others had been curious and friendly. She'd already made some friends, going out to coffee, getting tips about quirky furniture shops far beyond the designer boutiques and exclusive decorators of the Upper East Side.

In search of new furniture, Ruby had traveled downtown, then to Brooklyn, then even farther afield to villages on the Hudson River. Ruby's days had been filled with the joy of the hunt, finding one amazing piece after another to decorate their home.

It helped to keep busy. It was so strange not to have a job, or three. She sometimes didn't know what to do with herself.

But Ivy had finally answered her, as Ares had said she would. A week after he'd said that, her little sister had texted her.

Thanks for the college money. I just enrolled at Boise State.

Now the sisters talked regularly. Ruby hoped to have Ivy visit over the holidays, about the time her baby was due.

Standing in the center of the nursery, where she was folding little baby socks, Ruby looked down at her belly. Less than three months until their child would be born. She was happy.

She *was*.

Really.

Except...

Setting down the tiny socks, Ruby took a deep breath, rolling back her shoulders. She looked bleakly out the big window, which was flooded with morning light.

Ares still avoided talking about the baby. Although he'd allowed her to create the nursery and to buy things for their daughter, he'd never again gone to a doctor's visit. And whenever she brought up the subject, he would withdraw—first verbally, and if she persisted, he would literally get up and leave the room.

At least we never have arguments, she tried to comfort herself. But that was its own problem.

There are some things I cannot offer you. She could still hear his cold voice. *Love. Marriage. And we both know I won't be much of a father.*

Biting her lip, Ruby blinked back sudden tears. When Ares had taken her in his arms the night of that first gala and told her he wanted her to stay, she'd thought he'd changed. That he might be willing to actually have a relationship, if not a marriage. That he might want to be a real father to their child.

She wiped her eyes. She should be grateful. She had a beautiful home. A man who was very willing to provide a comfortable life for all of them, her sister included.

The trouble was, though she appreciated no longer having to worry about having food and a roof over their heads, a life of luxury wasn't what Ruby cared about. And after so many days in his company, so many nights in his arms, she'd come to think of him as a friend. As her best friend, even.

She'd seen a side of Ares that he kept secret from the rest of the world. He encouraged her. He could be funny, even kind. He could be vulnerable. He tried to hide it, but he couldn't. Not from her.

Not when she—

Ruby sucked in her breath.

Oh, my God.

She loved him.

Not just for the way he worshipped her in the hot darkness of night. Not just for his baby inside her. Not for the home he'd given her or the way he was constantly trying to spoil her.

Ruby loved him for the man he was inside, when no one else was looking. The man who cared, even when he tried not to. Even for her.

But Ares would never love her back. He'd told her from the beginning it wasn't in his nature. His past had burned love straight out of his soul.

A lump rose in her throat.

Hearing a single hard knock, she turned. Ares stood in the open doorway of the nursery, dressed in a sleek black suit and carrying a laptop bag.

His glance ran over her. "What's wrong?"

"Nothing." She tried to smile. "Just happy that this room's done." She changed the subject. "You're going to work?"

"Yes."

"But it's Saturday. I…I thought we could at least have breakfast together…"

"Sorry." Coming forward, he kissed her briefly. His eyes focused only on her, as if he were trying to ignore the crib and all the baby books and toys. "I'll be back late tonight." Leaning forward to nuzzle her cheek, he whispered, "Wait up for me."

"All right," she said, the pain in her throat becoming sharper. *She loved him.* The pressure of the realization was flooding through her body, making her shake with the effort it took not to blurt it out.

But as he turned to go, Ruby felt something that made her burst into a low, joyful laugh in spite of herself. A small sensation, like bubbles, inside her belly.

Ares turned back with a frown. "What?"

"Give me your hand!" Grabbing his hand, she put it across her belly, beneath both of her own. "The baby's kicking. Right there, feel it?" She gave him a broad grin. "She's either going to be a football player or a ballerina!"

For a split second, an expression of wonder crossed Ares's hard, handsome face. His lips parted in shock as he looked down at her belly. "That's her?"

"Yes," Ruby whispered, loving the look on his face. Loving that, for the first time, he seemed interested in the baby. Loving *him*.

Emotion built and swelled inside her, lifting up her heart until she couldn't breathe unless she said the words aloud. She tried to keep them inside. But she couldn't.

"I love you," Ruby whispered.

Ares looked up, his face blank.

"I love you," she repeated, unable to stop herself. "I tried not to. But I do. I love you..."

A shutter went over his expression. His dark eyes turned cold. He pulled his hand back.

"I have to go."

And he left.

As she stared after him, she realized what a horrible mistake she'd made. She never should have told him, ever. Raw pain gripped her heart. She held on to the crib so she didn't slide to the floor.

Mrs. Ford's cool voice came over the nursery's intercom. "There's a man here to see you, madam."

Numbly, Ruby pressed the button. "Who is it?"

"Braden Lassiter. He says he's here to say goodbye—shall I let him in the house?"

Braden. Her ex-fiancé from long ago, who'd abandoned her at the altar for his ice hockey career. Her heart's track record was abysmal, she thought. Maybe Ares was right to never let himself feel love. "Show him to the morning room."

Somehow, Ruby made it to the elevator and downstairs to the sunny room by the kitchen, overlooking the garden. As soon as she entered, Braden rose to his feet from the soft, comfortable sofa. He was tall and almost as broad shouldered as Ares, casually dressed in jeans and a T-shirt. "Hi, Ruby."

"Hi," she said wearily, already wishing he would go away so she could be alone with her misery. She felt like she was a million years old as she came toward him. Morning light left a soft golden haze on the comfortable furniture and the vintage chandelier with little bits of colored crystal shaped like fruit. She sank into the cushioned chair beside the sofa. "You're here to say goodbye?"

As he sat back down, the pro hockey player's face was wan. "I heard you were living in New York now. Having that rich guy's baby. I always meant to say hello once the season started." He shook his head. "But the season's already over for me. I just found out they're cutting me from the team."

"Cutting you?" She put her hands to her mouth. "Oh, no. Braden. Why?"

"I guess I wasn't good enough."

Leaning forward, she took his hand. "I'm so sorry. I know what it meant to you…"

"I knew you'd make me feel better. You always did." Braden gave her a crooked smile. "At least I have money saved up. I can go back to Star Valley and be a ski bum. The funny thing is…" He looked at her mournfully. "I always figured if I ever went back, Ruby, you'd be there, waiting for me."

Staring at him, she drew back her hand. "Braden…"

"You don't have to say it. I already know. You're not with this guy for his money. I kind of hoped you were. I could compete with that. But you love him. Don't you?"

Her eyes flooded with tears as she nodded. She couldn't speak over the lump in her throat.

"A lot?"

"Yes," she whispered. The pain in her throat became a razor blade. "But he doesn't love me. Or the baby. And he never will."

Braden suddenly scowled. "Why would you stay with him, then?" He moved forward, his gaze fierce. "You don't have to put up with it. There are lots of people at home who love you. Come back with me."

"What?" She gave a shocked laugh. "I'm pregnant with his baby."

"It doesn't mean he owns you." Braden lifted his chin. "You need a man who's not afraid to love you. Not afraid to be a father. Or a husband. Come back with me." He leaned forward. "I was young and stupid to ever let you go. If you ever gave me another chance—"

A hard sound echoed through the morning room as a laptop bag hit the marble floor. Ruby and Braden both whirled around guiltily.

Ares stood in the doorway, his eyes dark with fury.

For a moment, all Ares could hear was the pounding of his heart and the loud rush of blood through his veins as he looked at the hockey player sitting in *his* house and making a play for *his* woman. His vision turned red.

Hands tightening into fists, he stepped forward.

"No! Please!" Ruby cried, rising between the two men. "Don't!"

Hearing her voice, his vision cleared just enough to focus on her beautiful face. Her big brown eyes were pleading, her cheeks rosy with guilt. She was pleading for the other man? For that bastard hockey player who was trying to steal what was Ares's by right?

You need a man who's not afraid to love you. Not afraid to be a father. Or a husband. Come back with me.

Rage built inside him. He could feel his veins popping in his neck. He looked at Ruby, standing between them. Her curvaceous body, ripe with pregnancy, was half hidden beneath her bright yellow sweatshirt and pink jeans. The expression on his face must have been grim, because Ruby had a terrified look in her eyes.

"Please don't," she whispered, still holding up her hands as she stood between them in the cozy morning room. Ares looked at her incredulously.

"You're protecting him?"

"I don't need protecting," the hockey player responded, rising to his feet. "I wasn't telling her anything I wouldn't say to your face, Kourakis. If you can't love her or marry her, Ruby deserves a man who will."

It was all Ares could do not to grab one of the brightly colored lamps and smash his face with it.

"Please, Braden." Ruby turned to him. "Just go."

"Fine. I'm going." The man's gaze softened.

"Take good care of yourself, Ruby. I'll be in Star Valley."

And the burly hockey player left, giving Ares a wide berth. With good reason. Fury was pounding through his body. Hockey players were always losing teeth, weren't they? It took all of Ares's self-control not to knock out a few more.

Once the man was gone, he turned on Ruby.

"Why was he here?"

"He just got cut from his team. He was coming to say goodbye."

"He was begging you to run away with him!"

Ruby lifted her chin. Her eyes glittered. "That would shock you, wouldn't it? That any man would actually be willing to commit to me?"

Ares took a deep breath.

The morning had been one long disaster. First, there'd been a last-minute problem with negotiations over an acquisition in Italy, requiring him to go into the office when he would have far preferred to laze the morning away with Ruby in bed.

Then he'd felt the baby kick. That had brought a rush of emotions he couldn't deal with.

And as the final straw, Ruby had told him she loved him.

I love you. I tried not to. But I do. I love you.

He'd never wanted Ruby's love. Never asked for it. Women had told him they loved him before. He'd laughed it off.

This was different. He'd never expected how his body would react to hearing Ruby say those words.

His heart had pounded in his throat. His brain had spun. He'd broken out in a cold sweat. His body had reacted as if he'd been attacked by some dangerous, deadly foe. He'd stumbled out of the nursery feeling the cold steel of a sharp blade at his throat.

Ares couldn't let himself be seduced. He couldn't let himself love her back. That path could only lead to weakness. To pain. To destruction.

Love?

He'd lied when he said he didn't know what it was. He knew exactly what it was. *Love* was the word people used to manipulate. The word they used to hurt. To get what they wanted. To inflict maximum damage on their victims.

His father had used the word sparingly, and only when speaking of his horses, his dogs or his football club. Ares didn't know if the man had ever said it to his mistresses, but he doubted it. He certainly hadn't said it to his wife. Or his son.

His mother had used the word related to her child

only once, and that had been in an interview to
the press: *My son is away at boarding school. I
love him so.* Ares, only twelve and lonely in his
dorm room, had hugged that magazine close to his
skinny chest. But when he'd returned to Europe
at the next school break, his mother had treated
him just as she always had. *Ares, you're useless!
So selfish, just like your father! I can't stand the
sight of you!*

Love was Melice, lying to his face as she collected money from his father. It was Diantha promising fidelity while giving her virginity to another.

Love meant lowering your guard, and letting
your enemy inside your walls so they could set you
on fire at your weakest point: your heart. Leaving
only a crumpled heap of ash and bone.

In the face of Ruby's attack, Ares had fled the
nursery. But as Horace had driven him to the office, Ares couldn't stop thinking about it.

Love.

Ruby loved him.

Restless, he'd clawed back his hair, staring out
the back seat window. He didn't want to hurt her.
He'd seen her watching him with bewildered sadness as he'd avoided the nursery and refused to go
with her to the doctor. She didn't understand why

he didn't want to feel emotionally tied. Not to her. Not to the baby.

But this…

He couldn't get the image out of his mind of Ruby's pale, haunted face as she'd told him she loved him. And he'd left her without a word.

"Take me home," he'd told Horace hoarsely.

He didn't know what he would say to her. He'd only known he couldn't leave her like that, so lonely and broken.

Then he'd found her practically in another man's arms, as the man had begged for the chance to love her. Lonely and broken indeed!

Jaw clenched, Ares glared at Ruby.

"If you want to go marry him, nothing's stopping you," he ground out. It was a low hit, but the emotion inside him that he was repressing so intensely had to lash out. He heard her intake of breath.

Ruby came closer to him in the soft, sunlit room. "Why are you like this?"

"Like what?"

"I thought we were happy…"

"We are," he bit out.

"Then why did it make you so angry when I told you that I love you?" Her brown eyes were luminous. "Why do you hate it when I talk about our baby? Why do you keep pushing me away?"

Ares didn't answer.

With an intake of breath, she closed her eyes.

"Maybe you were right," she whispered. "This isn't going to work."

He looked up, shocked.

Ruby's face was pale and infinitely sad. "I was so happy when you asked me to stay. I thought it meant we might actually have a chance to be happy. To be a *family*. But now..." She looked around the morning room, which she'd redecorated so lovingly. "What was the point of fixing up this house when I'm not even part of your life?"

"You're part of it," he said harshly.

She gave a small smile. "At night I am. But during the day...I'm not your wife. I'm not even your girlfriend. You don't love me." Her voice cracked. "And you certainly don't love our child."

Part of him had always known she'd leave. It was one of the reasons why he couldn't let himself really care. He should just let her go.

And yet...

"I want you to stay," he said.

"Stay? You can't tell me to stay like I'm your pet. I need more. I'm in love with you, Ares." She gave a bitter laugh. "To you, my life is an open book. But you're so guarded. So hidden." She looked at him. "Maybe sex and money really is all you can offer any woman."

She was going to leave, he realized. His mind scrambled for ideas to make her stay. Something that would give her the illusion of what she wanted: his love.

Then he knew.

A flash of fear gripped him. He grimly pushed it aside.

It would just be a piece of paper. That was what everyone said, didn't they? But it would be a piece of paper that would bind her, so no other man could take her. Unlike his own parents, he knew Ruby valued marriage. Once the vows were spoken, she would never break them. No matter how cold or distant Ares might be in the future.

His fear of tying himself down vanished in his sudden determination to make sure *she* was tied down permanently. To him.

He turned to her. Ruby looked sad and small, her shoulders hunched, her eyes still red with crying.

But he could fix this. He would cancel all his business plans for the next week. Let his CFO deal with the headache of negotiating Kourakis Enterprises's acquisition in Milan. He had an urgent personal acquisition of his own.

Ares reached for her. "Ruby…"

She stepped back, not letting him touch her. "You don't love us. You never will." Her voice was heavy with unshed tears. "There's no reason for me to stay."

"Let me give you a reason," he said huskily, pulling her into his arms, though she tried to resist. Lowering his lips to hers, he kissed her. She stiffened, drawing back. Then she sighed against his mouth in surrender and her hands gripped his shoulders, drawing him closer. Even angry, she could no more resist the fire between them than he could.

Drawing back from their embrace, he whispered against her lips, "I want to show you something."

She gave a low, breathless laugh. "I bet you do."

Running his hands through her hair, he kissed her forehead, her cheeks. "You need to pack."

She blinked. "Pack? For what?"

"Bring a bikini."

"Where are we going?"

"You said you wanted to know me," he said roughly. He searched her gaze. "Let me take you to the place where I was born."

Staring at him, she gave a hesitant nod.

Triumph rushed through him. If the thought of marriage made him a little queasy inside, he firmly pushed the feeling away. It was the only way to keep her.

And he would. Dangerous or not. She belonged to him now. He'd been fooling himself to think he could send her away.

He would keep her. At any price.

CHAPTER TEN

THE HOT GREEK sun beat down on Ruby's skin a few days later as she stretched lazily in the soft lounge chair. She blinked, yawning like a kitten. Beside her chair an infinity pool shimmered blue, with a sheer drop-off overlooking the bright blue Ionian Sea.

Behind her, the Kourakis house loomed.

House? Ruby shook her head, amused at herself for using such an ordinary word for a place as big as a fortress and fancier than a palace, in a compound on a private island. The enormous villa shone blindingly white beneath the bright blue sky. She had to put on sunglasses to look at it directly.

It had been built by his grandfather, the first shipping tycoon, Ares had told her. His grandfather had started the family business in Athens, and Aristedes, Ares's father, had expanded it. But it had been Ares's ruthless, single-minded focus on Kourakis Enterprises that had turned it into a global empire.

"That's why I work so much," he'd confided with a lazy grin yesterday, twirling a tendril of her hair, as both of them snuggled naked in bed. "I always have to win. Even against my own ancestors."

She'd grinned back. Then her smile had faded. "You even compete against your own family?"

He'd stopped twirling her hair.

"Yes, Ruby," he'd said quietly. "You know the myth about the Greek god Zeus?"

"The leader of the gods?"

"He only survived childhood because his mother hid him from his father before he could devour him, as he had the rest of Zeus's siblings. Every generation competing against the next. That's what family is to me. Win or die. Eat or be eaten."

She'd tried to smile. "But not every family is like that. People usually love each other. Watch each other's backs. Keep each other safe."

His shoulders had relaxed, and he'd lowered his head to hers, whispering, "Maybe in your world…"

"So join my world," she'd whispered against his lips, and he'd kissed her.

They'd made love in the villa's master bedroom, near the open balcony overlooking the sea, as the waves crashed loudly below. He'd made her cry out so loudly with pleasure she'd blushed afterward, wondering if the staff of twelve that serviced the island might have heard her. Ares had snickered at her for being so concerned.

"They're discreet. Believe me. Some of them have worked here decades, and my parents' screaming at each other taught them to wear ear-plugs."

She'd given him a quick, worried look. "Was I screaming?"

He'd grinned at her. "Don't worry. Happy sounds will be a novelty for them."

"But surely you've brought women here before."

Shaking his head, he'd leaned forward, whispering, "You're the first…"

And he'd kissed her softly, and a sensual hour later, made her cry out all over again.

Now Ruby stretched in the sun, wiggling her toes, which had been painted red by the team of stylists and masseuses that had visited the island yesterday. As distractions went, she thought, whisking a girl away via private jet to a private Greek island was a pretty solid choice.

Ruby bit her lip. But a distraction was all it was. Because what could Ares possibly show her here that would change things between them? What could possibly give her hope that they even had a future?

Pushing the depressing thought away, Ruby closed her eyes beneath her sunglasses, turning her face toward the sun, her fingertips trailing into the cool water of the pool.

A shadow fell over her. "Enjoying yourself?"

Looking up, she saw Ares standing beside her lounge chair. She lowered her sunglasses.

The sun was shining behind his head, casting his dark hair with gold. He looked overwhelmingly sexy, in a loose white linen shirt and dark board shorts slung low on his hips. "So you do wear shorts."

"Don't tell anyone."

"It'll be our secret."

His dark eyes roamed over her body hungrily. "I like your bikini today."

Her lips quirked. "You like *all* my bikinis."

Sitting beside her on the lounge chair, Ares kissed her hello, as he'd done on the island whenever they were out of each other's sight for longer than ten seconds. His hands moved sensually over her bare skin, warmed by the sun. It was a long time later when he finally drew back from their embrace and asked, "Will you have a drink with me?"

Her lips quirked. "Such a formal invitation."

Ares didn't smile back.

She cleared her throat. "Inside the house?"

His expression was serious. "On the beach."

"Sure." Trying to understand his change in mood, Ruby was suddenly afraid he was going to tell her something she didn't want to hear. Something that would break her heart. She said through numb lips, "I'll just get my cover-up."

The sun was starting to lower into the western horizon, leaving streaks of red and orange across the wide sky and darkening sea, as he led Ruby, her bikini now covered by a white cotton caftan, down to the beach. The tide was going out, but though it was late September, the air was warm.

Ares held her hand as they walked in a direction they'd never gone on the beach before. His hand seemed to grip hers tighter. Then she stopped, her eyes wide.

A table set for two had been set up on the beach. Two smiling, uniformed staff members waited beside it expectantly.

Ruby looked at Ares. His lips lifted. "Our own little taverna."

Leading her to the table, he pulled out her chair on the hard-packed sand. As one servant poured drinks—sparkling water with lemon for her, and a glass of ouzo for him—the other lifted a silver lid off his tray to reveal a platter of appetizers, Greek olives, fresh vegetables, roasted nuts and vine leaves stuffed with rice. With a bow and another smile, the two waiters departed.

The butterflies in Ruby's stomach were turning into boulders. Her nervousness only increased as Ares's dark gaze caught hers.

"I have something to tell you," he said quietly, reaching for her hand across the table.

Ruby swallowed. She'd feared as much. "What?"

"I lied to you."

For a moment, she just stared at him. She heard the cries of seagulls flying above and the roar of the waves beating against the shore as the lowering sun reflected brilliantly off the sea.

"Lied?" Her voice cracked. "What do you mean?"

"When I told you I'd never been in love. I have." Ares paused. "Twice."

Ruby's stomach twisted. She'd thought he couldn't love anyone. But he'd loved two women who weren't her?

Taking a drink of his ouzo, he said, "After I

graduated from boarding school, I went to Paris to visit my mother. I hadn't seen her in four years." He paused. "She was too busy having an affair with her tennis instructor to care. But my first afternoon in the city, I met a girl."

"A girl?" Ruby said, unwillingly jealous. He gave a cynical smile.

"A beautiful *parisienne*, five years older than I was. Glamorous, worldly and wise. She said she was a fashion student. She told me she loved me almost at once. I'd never heard those words before, so I believed her. I convinced myself I loved her, too. And I suppose I did."

Ares looked back at the sprawling white villa clinging to the top of the green-forested cliff. His lips twisted.

"As a child, I swore I'd be different from my parents. I was idealistic. I didn't want to have sex until I knew I was really, truly in love."

Ruby nearly fell out of her chair. "You what?"

"I was eighteen." He gave her a crooked grin. "After a blissful summer with Melice, I found out she was a prostitute my father had hired to teach me the truth about women. He wanted me to be a man, he said. And stop thinking love was real or, as he put it, acting like a damned weakling."

Ruby stared at him, aghast. She couldn't even imagine how awful Ares's childhood had been, in spite of being so rich. Her heart twisted to think of him as a boy, lonely on this private island, surrounded by paid staff with two selfish monsters as his family and role models.

Ares gave a low, sardonic laugh. "You should see your face right now."

Breathing the sea air, she tried to smile. "And here Ivy thought all she had to do was get knocked up and you'd instantly fall in love with her."

He snorted. "I'm a more difficult mark than that, I'm afraid."

"I know." She tried to keep the bitterness from her voice.

Ares turned toward Ruby. The red sunset glowed like blood against his cheek. "You know better than anyone."

"I never saw you as a mark."

"That's what made you different." He took another drink, looking out at the waves against the nearby shore. "After that, it was too late to save myself for love, so I threw myself into one-night stands at university, with women too busy with their own lives to care about mine. But visiting Athens the summer before senior year, I met a girl so innocent and sweet, she reminded me of my old dreams. I quit sleeping around and planned to marry Diantha as soon as I graduated."

He stopped, staring out at the waves.

"What happened?" she said softly, though she already guessed.

"My father died unexpectedly a few weeks before graduation…"

Tears filled Ruby's eyes as she remembered how she'd felt when her own mother had died. She whispered, "I'm sorry."

"Don't be. He died of a heart attack while drinking and taking drugs trying to simultaneously satisfy two women in his bed." He tilted his head thoughtfully. "All things considered, I think it's how he would have wanted to go."

Ruby's mouth was wide. Looking at her, he gave another low laugh, then poured himself another drink from the ouzo bottle.

He took a gulp of his drink. "Rushing to Athens to seek the comfort of my beloved, I found my sweet, honest virgin naked in the arms of another man."

"Oh, no," she breathed.

Setting his glass down on the table, he looked at her. "If my father hadn't died, I never would have known. I would have married Diantha, even if my parents disinherited me for it. I would have been willing to sacrifice everything for love." He gave her a crooked smile. "I thought that was what love meant."

Ruby took a deep breath. "I'm sorry—"

He cut off her sympathy with a hard gesture.

"I never forgot that lesson. My parents were right all those years, teaching me not to care." He looked away. "I inherited everything. The company. The wealth. This island." He gave her a cynical smile. "The whole Kourakis legacy."

Reaching across the table, Ruby put her hand over his. She repeated helplessly, "I'm sorry."

"I wanted you to understand." Ares looked down at her hand. "Who I really am."

"I get it," she said over the lump in her throat.

His dark eyes pierced hers. "I haven't trusted anyone for most my life," he said in a low voice. "I've never wanted to try to love again. Or commit." His dark gaze burned through her in the twilight. "Until now."

It took several seconds for this to sink in. She breathed, "What?"

"I want to try." Reaching out, he tucked a dark

tendril of her hair behind her ear. "Perhaps I'll learn to love you. Over time."

Ruby's mind was spinning. Was this how it was supposed to be? He would learn to love her? Something inside her shrank at the thought. But if this was the best Ares could do, shouldn't she accept? And be grateful? "And our baby?"

"Her, too." He tilted his head. "But now you know the worst about me. I wouldn't blame you for running far and fast. Why would you want to marry a man like me? To tell you the truth, I think you deserve better."

Shocked tears lifted to her eyes. "Marry...?"

Sitting across from her at the small table on the edge of sea, Ares stared at her for a long moment. Then he rose from his chair.

She stared, wide-eyed, as he fell to one knee before her, as the waves of the sea pounded against the sand below.

Reaching into the pocket of his beach shorts, Ares withdrew a small black box. The sunset streaked violent shades of scarlet and purple against the sky as, opening the black velvet box, he held it up.

"Will you marry me, Ruby?" he asked quietly.

The diamond inside was dazzling. It was as big as an iceberg. But she didn't care about the ring.

Lifting her gaze to his handsome face, Ruby felt her heart in her throat. *Yes, oh, yes.* To be Ares's wife, now and forever? It was all she wanted. No matter how she'd tried to deny it. She wanted to be married to the man she loved, the man whose child she carried deep inside her. She wanted it more than she'd ever wanted anything in her life.

"Yes," she whispered.

He rose to his feet. "Yes?"

"Yes!" She flung her arms around him. For a long moment, they held each other. They stood on the beach together until the sun finally fell beyond the distant horizon, like a melting ball of fire.

Only the violet streaks remained across the fading twilight of the private Greek island, and the dark scarlet of the Ionian Sea, as he finally slid the ring over her finger.

Tearfully, she hugged him to her, kissing his cheeks, his lips. Wrapping his arms around her more tightly, he deepened their kiss into a long embrace.

But as he kissed her, the memory of his words intruded on her joy.

Perhaps I'll learn to love you. Over time.

Fiercely, Ruby pushed her uneasiness away. They'd be happy. They *would*. Ares would learn to love her; he'd said it himself. If not, she could love him enough for both of them.

But even as Ruby kissed him passionately, the huge, platinum-set diamond felt heavy and cold on her hand.

Ruby stared at herself in the mirror.

"You look so beautiful," her little sister breathed, peeking behind her. Ivy's eyes were filled with tears. "I can't believe you're getting married today."

Ruby took a deep breath. Her long dark hair was curled in long ringlets, courtesy of Ivy, and decorated with tiny pink roses. She'd done her own makeup. Ares had offered to call an entire team of stylists, if she'd wanted, but Ruby preferred to do it herself. Wanda, the owner of her favorite vintage shop in the Meatpacking District, had helped her choose a beaded cream dress as her wedding gown.

In the three days since they'd returned to New York, Ruby had thrown together a simple wedding. Nothing fancy, just a small ceremony attended by a few friends, including Ivy, who'd been whisked from Idaho via Ares's private jet. Flowers had been ordered from the shop on the corner. Mrs. Ford was doing the food. And as for the venue...

A smile lifted Ruby's lips. Finally, the mansion's ballroom would actually be useful.

Holding out the bridal bouquet of pink roses, Ivy wiped her tears with her shoulder. "I just wish Mom could be here."

Ruby took the bouquet, her eyes welling in turn. "So do I."

"Maybe she is." Ivy gave her a tearful smile. "When I think of that ridiculous plan I once had to seduce Ares, just because I was worried about our bills..." She shook her head. "I was a fool. Thank you for stopping me. But at least one good thing came of it. He got the chance to meet you. And now I'm going to be an auntie." She looked fondly at Ruby's belly. "Someday I hope to fall madly, recklessly in love like you."

"You do?"

"I can hear your love for him in your voice, every time you say his name. And I'm sure he feels the same. You'd never settle for less."

Ruby felt a chill beneath the beautiful wedding gown. "Um."

"I'm so happy. No one deserves love more." Her

little sister hugged her fiercely. "I'll see you after the ceremony."

After Ivy headed downstairs to join the other guests, Ruby took a deep breath, looking at herself one last time in the bedroom mirror. Next time she returned here, she would be Mrs. Ares Kourakis.

"He'll learn to love me," she told herself fiercely. "Everything will be fine."

But her reflection didn't look so sure.

Skipping the elevator, Ruby walked slowly down the stairs in her chic little white booties, one flight after another, trying to calm her pounding heart. *He will love me*, she repeated to herself as she walked. *I know he will.*

She stopped in the doorway of the gorgeous high-ceilinged ballroom, decorated with flowers. Then, with a deep breath, she entered, holding her head high.

The small group of guests—her sister; Ares's assistant, Dorothy; Mrs. Ford; Horace; Georgios and his family; the rest of the house staff; and Ares's friend from school, a hotel billionaire called Cristiano Moretti—all rose to their feet, staring at her approvingly. "Beautiful," someone murmured, as a musician started playing "Wedding March" on acoustic guitar.

But to Ruby, there was only one person who mattered. She beamed when she saw Ares at the center of the ballroom, standing next to the minister. But why did his face look so pale and strange?

Ruby hesitated, then, squaring her shoulders, walked down the flower-strewn aisle, holding her bouquet. Guests whispered words to her as she passed, words of encouragement and praise.

But when she reached Ares, she knew that something was seriously wrong. His handsome face was white beneath his tanned skin. His dark eyes looked hollow, as if something had cracked deep inside. He looked so pale. No sign of life at all.

He looked, she thought suddenly, like he was already dead.

Why would you want to marry a man like me? To tell you the truth, I think you deserve better.

Ruby stopped, clutching her bouquet of pink roses as everything became clear.

Ares didn't do complicated. He'd told her that, long ago, when he hadn't wanted to meet her dying mother or the little sister who'd hoped to seduce him. He didn't like complicated. And what could be more complicated than family? What could be more complicated than marriage, or raising a child?

He didn't love her. He was still going to marry her. He would settle. Because he didn't want to lose her.

Ruby stared at the bleak expression on his handsome face. Ares was clearly forcing himself to go through with this. The man of her dreams was choking her down as if she was an unpalatable dose of medicine.

The music stopped. From six feet away, Ares frowned at her when she didn't move. His face was like a stranger's. "Ruby?"

She put her hands to her head. Her heart was beating so fast. The world was spinning around her, the colors of the ballroom, the flowers, the bright dresses of their friends.

Perhaps I'll learn to love you. Over time.

And our baby?

Her, too.

What would that do to her sweet daughter's soul, to be raised by a man who had to be forced to love her?

Ruby looked up.

"I can't do this."

She heard a gasp from the guests behind her.

His expression hardened. *"Ruby."*

"I can't," she whispered, clutching the pink roses.

Her heart was howling. "This—this isn't how it's supposed to be."

"It's everything I can give," he said tightly.

"I know." After these last few months, she'd never imagined she could refuse to marry Ares if he asked her. Not in a million years. But she couldn't force him into a marriage without love. Not when, to him, it must look like a prison sentence.

He'd been right all along.

Ruby deserved better.

Their baby deserved better.

And so, even, did he.

Trembling, she took the last steps toward him. She heard a soft whoosh and crunch beneath her feet and realized she'd dropped her bouquet and smashed it into the marble floor. Crushed pink roses trailed behind her.

Reaching up, Ruby tearfully lifted her hand to his rough cheek. He didn't move. His dark eyes looked numb.

"Be happy," she whispered. Tears overflowed her lashes, streaking down her cheeks. Before she started to sob, she turned and fled the ballroom.

Alone in the empty hallway, Ruby rushed past the double staircase for the foyer. She couldn't bear to remain, not even long enough to go upstairs and gather her clothes. Going to the front closet, she swept up her canvas bag with her wallet and phone, the same one that she'd brought from Star Valley all those months ago.

"Ruby!" Her sister stumbled out of the ballroom. "Wait!"

She looked back one last time at the nineteenth-century mansion she'd redecorated with such love and hope. This house had felt so wrong at first. Then she'd fallen in love with it. She'd given her heart to it recklessly, never thinking she might someday lose it. So brutally. So...permanently.

She closed her eyes.

I love you, Ares. I'll love you forever.

Turning, she headed for the front door. She stepped through, with her sister following close behind, out into the gray October morning.

Ruby looked back at the house one last time, feeling numb, like she was about to fall apart. But she couldn't. She put her hands softly around her baby bump. She had to be strong. Setting her jaw, she lifted her arm to hail a taxi on the street. And then, just like that, they were gone.

Ares stood at the window of his executive office at the top of his Midtown high-rise. The city beneath looked cold, covered by a blanket of late January snow. But not half as cold as he felt.

His jaw tightened as he glanced back at his desk. An open package rested on two newspapers brought in that morning by his assistants, along with the rest of his mail. Inside the package was a note from Ruby.

This belongs to you.

It was attached to the enormous diamond platinum-set engagement ring that he'd given her on the beach at twilight, beneath the shadow of his family's Greek villa. He could still remember his satisfaction when she'd said yes, and he thought he'd won.

He'd told her the worst thing about his soul. He'd told her he didn't know if he could ever love her or the baby. She'd still said yes.

And then she'd abandoned him at the altar. In front of everyone. He'd offered her everything he knew how to give. It still hadn't been enough.

Ares closed his eyes. Even after nearly four months, he could still hear Ruby's sweet voice and joyful laugh. Still feel her full red lips and soft body against his own. Still see her beautiful face. Still remember the stricken anguish in her luminous dark eyes on their wedding day. Her eyes had pierced his soul, and in that moment, he'd known he'd been judged and found wanting.

I can't. This—this isn't how it's supposed to be.

His heart contracted, and Ares pressed his fist against the glass. He'd managed to repress all emotion since she'd walked out on him. But now, as that diamond engagement ring gleamed wickedly in the artificial light of his office, he suddenly could no longer force down the raw pain.

He'd felt numb before the wedding, sick at the thought of marriage. But he'd forced himself to go through with it, because his only other option was to lose her.

Then she'd left.

His friends had crowded around him in the ballroom, bewildered by the turn of events, trying to offer comfort. Of all the guests, Cristiano Moretti was the only one who had a bad word to say about Ruby, and of course, he hadn't known her. But he'd taken Ares out to get drunk and to trash Ruby's character. Now, that was a real friend, he thought. Though heaven knew Cristiano had issues of his own.

The next morning, Ares had woken up with a splitting headache and a sense of despair. Noth-

260 CLAIMING HIS NINE-MONTH CONSEQUENCE

ing was wrong with Ruby's character. Her greatest flaw was that she'd seen right through him.

And now that she was gone, even his own home seemed to mock him. Her ridiculously bright clothes still hung in his closet, along with her scent, her colors, her memory everywhere.

Ares had immediately ordered everything in the house to be changed back to the way it was, with stark black-and-white furniture. He'd ripped out the baby's nursery, with its happy pink walls and the toys and books Ruby had collected so joyfully. The pink walls became gray and the crib was sent back. He'd told Mrs. Ford to toss the stuffed animals into the trash.

Instead, his mutinous housekeeper had sent them to Ruby in Star Valley. "They were just too precious to destroy," Mrs. Ford had said firmly. "The baby will still want them."

Incensed, Ares had fired her in a fury.

"You can't fire me," Mrs. Ford retorted, pulling off her apron, "because I quit! I won't work for a selfish fool!"

How could she accuse him of being selfish? Ares ground his teeth at the memory. He'd given everything he could. Ruby had still left.

And in the months since, she'd never contacted

him once. Three days before Christmas, that sister of hers had called him.

"Your daughter was born this morning at Star Valley General," Ivy told him breathlessly. "Seven pounds, ten ounces. Both mother and child are doing well!"

"Thank you," he'd said, feeling panic. "I'll get there as soon as I can."

"No." Ivy's voice was awkward, even strangled. "I'm sorry, Ares, but…Ruby doesn't want you here."

Remembering, a fragment of ice lodged in his throat. His baby was a month old now. And he didn't even know her name.

He'd legally transferred ownership of the ski lodge to Ruby, as promised. For all the good it had done. After all this time, his caretaker hadn't seen her, not once. Even the hefty checks of financial support that Ares sent her each month had been deposited straight into their daughter's untouchable trust fund. Ares had no idea how Ruby was paying for her daily expenses.

It seemed even his money wasn't good enough, along with his name.

Sitting back heavily in his desk chair, Ares

looked down at the ring. The ostentatious diamond looked as cold and hollow as he felt.

Ruby had tried to love him. But that was too big a job for any woman, even one with a heart as generous as hers. He clawed back his hair. He'd hoped he could fool her with the illusion of love by making her his wife. By promising to try to love her someday, like someday there might be a colony on the moon. He should have known she would see right through that.

Maybe he was a fool after all.

His intercom buzzed.

"Miss Spencer is here, sir," his executive assistant said. "Should I send her in?"

Ares wondered what Poppy was doing at his office. He hadn't seen her since the night of the gala, when she'd shown off her punk rocker fiancé and tried her best to snub Ruby. "Yes."

The door of his private office burst open. Poppy Spencer stood in his doorway, dressed in a tight black cocktail dress and a sable fur coat, though it was only the midafternoon. Looking at him, she spread her arms dramatically as she walked into his office.

"Darling! I won't have it."

He was already tired of her being here. Setting

his jaw, he rose to his feet. "What do you want, Poppy?"

"I'm tired of you never showing up at social events anymore. You've been hiding long enough. I won't have it, I tell you." Poppy sat down in the chair in front of his desk, crossing her bare legs. She pulled a cigarette case out of her expensive crocodile handbag. "You're being ridiculous."

"You can't smoke that here," he said automatically, looking down at her.

"Don't be silly," she said, lighting it. "So the waitress broke your heart."

He ground out, "She didn't—"

"Whatever. Get over it." She waved out the match. "As it happens, I have had a similar disappointment."

"Your fiancé?"

"Took up with a groupie in Florida." Taking a puff, she looked at him coolly. "The problem is, darling, we've both of us made a habit of conducting affairs with unsuitable people."

The sound of her voice set his nerves on edge. "Unsuitable?"

She waved her cigarette. "They're below us. We choose them because we think they'll be easy to discard. And they are." She gave a tinkly crystalline laugh. "But it's a humiliation when they choose to leave us first."

Ares's heart was jagged in his throat. "I never thought of Ruby that way."

"Sure." Poppy looked up at him. "I have a solution. A simple, elegant solution that will make sure neither of us has such an embarrassment again." She took another puff. "You and I should marry."

Ares stared down at her incredulously. "What?"

Her red lips curved. "Think about it. We're the same, you and I."

"We're not."

"Of course we are. Neither of us is meant for commitment. To us, love is poison. We're both free spirits who value our freedom above all else."

"How can you say that? I am committed to my company. You change your careers with the season."

Poppy looked at him steadily, then took another elegant puff of her cigarette. "We both fill our days to avoid feeling anything we don't want to feel."

Ares stared at her.

Had he done just that, filling his life with endless work and forgettable one-night stands?

He'd been trying to avoid pain. He thought he'd learned how—by avoiding all feeling altogether.

No wonder he'd felt such emptiness. A loneliness he'd refused to admit, even to himself.

The night he'd met Ruby, he'd been drawn not just by her beauty, but by her warmth and passion for life. He'd been pulled to her like a freezing man to a fire.

Avoiding love hadn't even kept the pain away. That was the worst part. He took a deep breath. He hadn't let himself love Ruby, but after she'd left, no matter how he tried to deny it, he'd still been drowning in the misery of her loss.

Ares closed his eyes. From childhood, every time he'd loved someone, every single time, they'd hurt him. He'd decided as an adult that the lesson was well learned. He was done feeling pain ever again.

But there was no escaping pain. Trying to evade it, all he'd done was deny himself the possibility of joy. Since Ruby had gone, he'd lived in shadow, in a bleak half-life, without her sunlight. She was the sun to him.

Because he loved her.

Ares opened his eyes with a low, strangled curse. *He loved her.*

He'd convinced himself he couldn't love Ruby. That love had been burned out of his soul.

He was wrong.

All this time, he'd loved her. And he loved their baby. He always had.

"Darling, what is it?" Poppy said, rising to her feet. "You look so strange."

Ares looked around his executive office, at the elegant spare furnishings, at the papers and sleek computer, and sucked in his breath.

What the hell was he still doing here?

Grabbing Poppy by the shoulders, he kissed her hard on the cheek. "Thank you."

Turning away, he grabbed his wallet and a coat.

"What was that for?" Poppy cried, putting a hand to her cheek.

"You made me realize what I should have known long ago." Ares looked back at her from the open doorway, his whole being suddenly suffused with joy. "I love her."

"What?"

As he crossed the office with quick strides of his long legs, he yelled back, loud enough for the whole floor to hear, "I love her!"

Night had fallen by the time Ares's private jet landed at the small airport outside Star Valley. The Idaho mountains were jagged and snowy beneath the winter moonlight. A vintage Land Rover was already waiting for him on the tarmac.

"Thank you, Dorothy," he murmured aloud to no one. His breath swirled white in the frigid air. He'd called his assistant from the jet as he left New York and asked for her help. He needed people, Ares realized. The idea that any man could survive alone, without trusting anyone for all his life, was just stupid.

Would Ruby forgive him? Would she believe him when he said he loved her? He thought wretchedly of the handsome hockey player who so easily had offered everything that Ares could not. It had been nearly four months.

What if he was too late?

He already knew she wouldn't be at the ski lodge. But as he pulled in front of Ruby's trailer in her old neighborhood, his heart sank. It looked like no one had lived here for a long time.

"You looking for Ruby Prescott?" An old-timer peered from the next-door trailer into his SUV. "Slick truck you got there."

"Yes, do you know where she is?" Ares asked anxiously.

"At her new shop, I reckon. She and the baby live above it now. You can't miss it. Two-story brick building downtown. Next door to that infernal Atlas Club."

The old man was right. Ares couldn't miss it. As he drove through downtown Star Valley, he saw a crowd of people on the sidewalk next to the Atlas Club, hanging out in the snowy night. But they weren't there to dance.

Ruby's Vintage Delight, a neon sign read above the neighboring door. Parking his SUV two blocks away, he pushed through the crowds into the shop.

Inside the large space, well-dressed people were smiling and laughing as musicians played live music. Colorful balloons covered the ceiling. As soon as he walked in, someone offered him a home-brewed bottle of root beer, and he recognized the young skiers from Renegade Night. Shaking his head, Ares looked around him, dazzled.

Ruby had done this. Vintage clothing hung on racks and against the brick walls, along with eclectic home decor. The boutique shone with warmth and color. Just like Ruby.

Then he saw her.

Ruby was wearing a 1950s-style red dress. Her long dark hair was pulled back by a red headband that matched her red lips. Her cheeks were rosy, her big brown eyes sparkling as she beamed at her friends standing around her. Then she laughed, kissing something that was snuggled in her arms.

Ares felt his heart in his throat.

The baby. His baby.

With an intake of breath, Ares pushed through the crowd. People fell back as they recognized him, and the whispers began just like always, just like they had back at the Atlas Club, the night they'd first met.

"Ares Kourakis..."

"He's here..."

"I knew he'd come for her..."

Ignoring them, he focused only on Ruby. As if she felt his gaze, her eyes met his.

Her smile dropped. Her beautiful face went blank.

Despair rushed through Ares's heart. He'd never seen her face so devoid of emotion before. He was too late. He'd waited too long. She'd given up on him. She'd found someone else, someone worthy of her. That was what she'd been trying to tell him when she sent back the ring.

"What are you doing here?" Ruby said.

She deserved to know, Ares thought bleakly.

Even if she no longer loved him back. But it was hard to speak the words.

Then the tiny baby in her arms gave a sneeze, and Ruby looked down and smiled, stroking her daughter's downy head. And all Ares could think was that he'd lost everything, everything that mattered a damn, because of his fear, denial and selfish pride.

Coming closer, Ares looked down at the baby. "She's beautiful."

"Yes," Ruby said in a low voice. "I love her."

He wanted to ask Ruby if she'd stopped loving him. But the words felt like a razor blade in his throat.

Ares looked at the shop around them. "This place is incredible. It reminds me of you."

Ruby blinked fast, then set her jaw. "Why are you here?"

Ares looked around the boutique, filled with color and joy and music. Filled with her friends. Filled with everything he'd never let himself want, because he'd been too busy protecting himself with walls of money. And in front of everyone, he turned to Ruby, and humbly spoke the words directly from his heart, loud enough for everyone to hear.

"Because I love you, Ruby. And I couldn't live another second without telling you. I love you."

Ruby had worked hard all her life. But the last four months had tested even her limits. And since her daughter had been born, she'd been getting by on fumes, sleeping at two-hour intervals. She'd never been so tired.

Or so proud. Tonight, she'd planned her vintage boutique's opening party to mark the end of one dream—her desperate love for a man who hadn't loved her back—and the celebration of another. A new dream she'd created for herself and her daughter.

For so many years, she'd dreamed of having her own little shop, but she'd been scared to try. What if she made a fool of herself? What if she failed?

But after doing both so spectacularly—loving Ares, and having her heart crushed so completely—when she'd returned to Star Valley nearly four months ago, she was no longer afraid.

Encouraged by Ivy and her friends, she'd started working for her dream. She'd learned how to start her own business, checking out books from the library, researching online. She'd written out a business plan and finally asked her friend Gus at the bank for a loan.

"About time, Ruby," Gus had chided with a shake of his red beard. "Dude. Everyone's been waiting for you to do this. You're going to make a fortune." Grinning, he'd rubbed his hands together. "And so will the bank."

Loan in hand, she'd sweet-talked her way into a lease in downtown Star Valley, with very good terms from the owner, her old boss Paul Vence, who still told her she was the best damn employee he'd ever had. The lease included an apartment on the second floor. She did much of the remodeling herself, but also got her friends to help for the price of beer and pizza. She'd hoped to open her shop in December, but that was delayed by the birth of her daughter. Bringing her baby home to a snug little apartment that was theirs, all theirs, with her business taking shape downstairs, had made it the best Christmas ever.

Almost.

If it had been hard not to think of Ares constantly, Ruby did her best. If she'd cried over him during the day, well, there was no one to hear and that had just made her polish the floors faster. If she'd cried over him at night, while rocking her baby to sleep, the stinging in her eyes just made her go to sleep all the sooner.

She could live without Ares's love. Because she had no choice.

But Ruby had feared what would happen if she saw Ares again. Her heart couldn't bear that. If he came to see the baby in the hospital, even for an hour, she'd been afraid she would totally lose the last shreds of her dignity by clinging to him and begging him not to leave. Begging him to tell her what she could do, who she had to be, to make him love her and their child.

So she'd told Ivy that she didn't want him to come. She was sure Ares would secretly be relieved. He'd sent money, which she'd tucked into Velvet's trust fund. The money was for their daughter.

Ruby was too proud to take money from a man who could not give her his love.

Yesterday, while doing the final touches for the party, she'd found the cold, heavy, heartless diamond she'd stuck deep into her sock drawer and known it was time to let it go. She'd sent back to him by overnight courier.

She prayed that would help her forget. That hot dreams of him would stop torturing her at night and agonizingly bittersweet memories stop haunting her by day.

The grand opening of Ruby's Vintage Delight would be the start of her new life. She'd told herself there was no more room for sadness now. Only joy.

All signs already pointed to her success. So many of Star Valley's citizens, both locals and out-of-towners, had begged for invitations tonight, she'd had to turn some away. The wife of a visiting Silicon Valley tycoon had already offered to help her expand, possibly to Deer Valley or Jackson Hole.

Ruby had said no. For now. She already had her hands full. Literally. She'd smiled down at her baby.

Then she'd seen Ares standing in her new life like a ghost.

Emotion had exploded in her chest, and Ruby had known she'd been lying to herself to think she could ever forget. No matter where she lived, no matter how many businesses or friends she had, she would carry love for him in her heart forever.

And as he stood beside her, looking down at their baby for the first time, Ruby looked at him in shock. He loved her?

She'd never, ever imagined this. Not in her wildest dreams.

"You—you love me?" she breathed. She shook her head. "But you said—"

"I know what I said. I was a fool." He paused, then said quietly, "I was a coward."

Looking at the dark unshaven scruff on his hard jawline, at the gray smudge beneath his eyes, Ruby wouldn't believe it. She shook her head.

"You'll never love anymore." Her arms tightened around Velvet, who was so tiny and sleeping peacefully against her chest. "Why are you really here?"

He pulled Ruby gently into his arms. "Because I've been living in hell without you. And it made me realize."

"What?"

His dark eyes met hers. "Nothing in my life is worth a damn without you, Ruby. My fortune—nothing. My empire—nothing. All that matters is you." He glanced down at the tiny sleeping newborn. "Both of you."

Ruby's lips parted in shock that Ares would say such a thing, and in front of so many strangers. A few people had sneakily pulled out smartphones, no doubt to post videos on the internet later. Ares didn't seem to care.

"But I was afraid to give you my heart," he whispered. "I thought that money, mansions, private jets and a diamond ring would be enough to hold you. While even that hockey player," he said in a low voice, "was brave enough to offer you everything." There was a strange sheen in his dark eyes as he looked at her. "Am I too late?"

Was he— No. Ares couldn't have tears in his eyes at the thought of losing her. It was impossible. "Too late?"

"After what I did, I wouldn't blame you," he said quietly. "If you chose to give your heart to another."

An incredulous laugh escaped Ruby. "Give my heart? To Braden?" She shook her head. "He was just scared of going back to Star Valley alone. He was barely here a week before he got another offer and promptly left for Calgary."

With an intake of breath, Ares searched her gaze. "So there's no one else?"

"Just my shop," she said, looking around her at the place she'd created, built with faith and friends and her own two hands. She looked down lovingly at her sleeping baby. "And Velvet."

The hard lines of his handsome face blurred into an incredulous grin. "Her name is Velvet?"

She raised her chin, waiting for him to tell her he hated it. "Velvet Kourakis."

He gave an intake of breath. "You gave her my name?"

"You said it was important to you," she said in a small voice. "And even though we weren't together, I couldn't betray that…"

Leaning forward, he put his hand tenderly on their sleeping baby's dark tufted head. He looked up, and his luminous gaze burned through her. "Thank you." He looked slowly around the boutique. "This shop is exactly like you. All warmth and joy." He blinked fast. "I wanted to give you my name, as well."

Ruby looked away. "I couldn't marry you." Her voice was low. "Not when I saw your face at the wedding. You looked sick at the thought of marrying me. I couldn't do that to you. Or to myself."

"You were right." He put his hand on her cheek. "Losing you forced me to realize that. You were right to leave me. You and the baby deserve more."

Tears filled her eyes. Now that she'd seen him again, she didn't want anyone else. She wanted only him.

"But I can be more," he continued in a low voice. "If you just give me a chance. I love you so much,

Ruby. If there's anything I can do to make you love me again…"

She looked up with an intake of breath.

"You can't," she said hoarsely. His dark eyes looked stricken.

Shaking her head, Ruby whispered with a tremulous smile, "Because I never stopped loving you."

Ares's hard-edged face filled with fierce joy as he searched her gaze. "You love me?"

Wordlessly, she nodded.

Pulling her closer, he choked out, "But I don't deserve it."

"No," she agreed.

"I was a selfish bastard."

"Yes." She paused. "But you have your finer points."

His dark eyes were shining. "I do?"

"Definitely," she whispered, putting her hand on his rough cheek. "Once you believe in something, Ares, you fight for it all the way. And you don't fight fair."

"Is that a good thing?"

"It is if you're fighting for us."

"I will always fight for you." Their eyes locked. Then, as if in slow motion, he fell to one knee before her.

There was a gasp across the vintage boutique. By now, everyone was holding up a smartphone.

Ares pulled a small black velvet box out of his dark cashmere coat.

"You brought back my ring?" Ruby said, creasing her forehead.

A smile lifted Ares's hard features, making his dark eyes almost merry as he said gravely, "Not quite."

After opening the box, he held up a small Edwardian-style ruby ring set in filigreed gold.

"A railway tycoon gave this ring to his bride in New York City a hundred and fifty years ago," he said huskily. "The owner of the jewelry shop told me they were happily married for half a century. That's what I want, Ruby. But fifty years isn't nearly enough. I want forever."

Her view of him shimmered with tears as she looked down at him over their sleeping newborn's head. He took the ring out of the box.

"Will you, Ruby?" Ares held up the ring, and now there could be no doubt. There were definitely tears in his eyes, too. "Will you give me forever?"

The whole shop seemed to hold its breath.

Ruby smiled as tears streamed down her cheeks. She whispered, "A thousand times over."

Joy lit up Ares's face as he slid the ring onto her finger. After rising to his feet, he took her and the baby in his arms, and Ruby knew, before he even kissed her, that a thousand times forever wouldn't even be long enough.

Their wedding was held in June in a sun-drenched flower meadow outside Star Valley, just below the peak of Mt. Chaldie.

The minister, an old friend of Ruby's mother, beamed between them as he spoke the last words of the ceremony. "You may now kiss the bride."

Ares looked at her. Ruby's dark hair, covered with a translucent lace veil embroidered with red flowers, was edged gold by the bright Idaho sun. She was wearing her mother's simple vintage dress of cream lace, and her beautiful face was transcendent with joy as she smiled up at him.

Their six-month-old baby was honorary flower girl, dressed in a sweet yellow cotton dress. Her proud aunt Ivy held her in her arms as Velvet wasn't walking yet. But the baby, chubby and happy, waved her arms wildly and gurgled a laugh, as if she knew her parents had just been wed.

Velvet wasn't the only one. As the summer wind

rattled softly through the trees, their friends and family, including Ruby's distant cousins from Coeur d'Alene, all cheered. And Ares wished he could freeze this moment in time and make it last the rest of his life. His wife's smiling face. Their baby's laugh. The gleam of sunshine against the gold rings they both now wore.

He blinked hard, trying to make a picture in his mind and heart he'd always remember. The day he'd gained happiness greater than he'd ever deserved.

"Kiss her!" one of their friends heckled. Ruby's smile widened as she looked up at him, her red lips trembling, her warm brown eyes shining with love.

Reaching out, Ares pulled his bride into his arms. "You've made me so happy."

"Me, too," she whispered.

"Not such a fool after all," called Mrs. Ford. His former housekeeper, upon hearing that Ares was back with Ruby, had immediately informed him that she would do him the privilege of working for him again. He'd brought her, along with other friends and staff members, to Star Valley for the wedding. He would even have invited Poppy, out of gratitude for her accidental help, if she wasn't already off sailing the world with her fencing instructor. What else was a private jet for?

He grinned at the housekeeper.

"Never a fool again," he vowed.

His wife put her hand in his. "We'll be fools together."

Ares's heart twisted with pride. Ruby's business was booming. Their child was thriving. The ski lodge had become a comfortable, colorful home. Last month, he'd even offered to officially move his company headquarters to Star Valley to support her.

But Ruby had refused. "I know you love New York," she'd said. "For you, it will always be the center of the world."

"Not anymore," he'd said huskily. "The center of my world is you."

With two separate businesses, they would split their time between New York and Star Valley, traveling always as a family. It would be complicated, he knew. But as their friends cheered in the sunny June afternoon, Ares could hardly wait for the mayhem to begin.

He'd lived a half-life before he met Ruby. A shallow, meaningless existence. Now, because of her, Ares finally knew what it felt like to be truly rich.

Not in money, but in things that actually mattered. A wife. Friends. A home. Family.

"I love you," Ruby whispered now, smiling, in happy tears as she looked up at him. He cupped her cheek.

"I will remember this moment for the rest of my life," he said in a low voice. "As the day my life began."

She tangled her fingers in his. "*Our* lives."

"Yes," he said over the lump in his throat. "Our lives." He gave her a sudden wicked grin. Leaning forward, he whispered in her ear, "By the way, I'm going to get you pregnant tonight."

Her gasp still rang in his ears as he ruthlessly covered her lips with his own. As the kiss deepened, she wrapped her arms around his shoulders. He heard cheering and applause. But in this moment, in this perfect kiss, it was just the two of them. Best friends, lovers. *Married.*

Their marriage began, blending all their past sorrows, all their future promise and strength. Life was complicated. Ares knew that now. There was no getting around it. It was rain and rainbows; darkness and sunshine. It was grief and joy and everything in between.

Ruby. Their baby. Their family.

On second thought, Ares realized, life wasn't complicated at all. Life was simple.

It was love.

* * * * *

LET'S TALK

Romance

For exclusive extracts, competitions
and special offers, find us online:

f facebook.com/millsandboon

⊙ @millsandboonuk

🐦 @millsandboon

Or get in touch on 0844 844 1351*

For all the latest titles coming soon,
visit millsandboon.co.uk/nextmonth